IN OLD PIMA COUNTY

Foster Campbell

ISBN: 1511431512
ISBN 13: 9781511431514
Library of Congress Control Number: 2016914412
CreateSpace Independent Publishing Platform
North Charleston, South Carolina

THIS BOOK IS DEDICATED TO MY
MOM AND DAD
FOR INTRODUCING ME
TO MY FIRST LOVE,
ARIZONA

CHAPTER 1

THURSDAY NIGHT

Everything changed when the tall Mexican entered La Cantina. Edwin Brody had spent all the late afternoon in the heat of the day, the worst part of the day, sitting at the teetering table and attempting to drink away the Bad Thought. He had done well; he was in an alcohol-induced stupor, and the plinking of the out-of-tune guitars and the one bleating trumpet had ceased to be a din and had become part of the distant background of noise. Very dark corn whiskey and a deep gouge in the table occupied his attention enough so that the Bad Thought had ceased to be a problem, for now. The poor Mexican farmers left him alone. He was nice enough when sober, and this gringo lawman was obviously fighting some demon. Sometimes they would see him sit in La Cantina and swat away an unseen menace the same way one would swat away a bothersome fly. Mostly, they noticed, he sat quietly and would roll one shoulder then the other, stretching his neck out as if he were uncomfortable in his own skin. Alcohol had turned plenty of nice men into killers, they knew. Why push this lawman? They chose to smile and nod in response to his smiles and nods. But they would not interact any further.

But the entrance of the big Mexican shook him into a new awareness. Brody studied the man and took in his look and demeanor. This man was dressed in green pants with silver conchos sewn to the outer seams. His vest had silver embroidery. No local could afford that dress in three lifetimes of work. The poor farmers who made up Fuerte Viejo were short, worn from hard labor, and dressed in plain white pants and shirts with little in the way of color. Clearly this was no farmer. He was too big, too tall, and too well dressed (though very dirty) to be a local or a family member visiting from down south. He might be a vaquero from the recent and few fledgling cattle ranches in the southern Arizona grasslands, but the thought crossed his mind that this man might be one of Los Hombres, one of the robbing land pirates that were the scourge of the vaqueros of the great haciendas and the cowboys of the first meager ranches of Arizona, the bane of Federales of the south and the marshals of the north. The man dropped a heavy coin on the plank that served as a bar and grabbed a bottle of something; Brody was too drunk to notice what.

Though his Spanish was poor, and he was very drunk, he could make out some of what the man said. "American bastards...corn growing...bank...O'Meara...gringo bastards...O'Meara..."

O'Meara! That was it! That was a problem, he knew, but his logic was so weakened by the alcohol that he could not reason why. Some innate sense told him that he had to grab this man before he rode out of town and disappeared. But like his logic, the senses of space and time were distorted as well. The Hombre seemed to wane and wax in distance though he was standing at the bar, and already Brody was unsure if the Mexican had been there for ten minutes or an hour. The time to act was now.

Slowly he staggered his way around the table and stood behind his victim, waiting for him to take another swig from the bottle. As the man tilted his head back, Brody drew his heavy Remington revolver and brought it in a high overhand arc down upon the man's head. The Hombre stood still momentarily before dropping his bottle and collapsing to the ground in a motionless heap. With eyes as glassy as if he himself had been knocked silly, Brody looked at the other patrons. They all nodded politely and smiled. "*Bueno,* Señor Edwin. Is good, is good."

CHAPTER 2
FRIDAY MORNING

The sun had been over the horizon for three hours when he finally made the effort to sit up in bed. He tried it slowly so that the ropes underneath would not rock or sway and make him more sick than he already was, or send him sprawling onto the dirt floor. His hangovers were different from what he had heard others' were like—no headache or aversion to loud noises, but rather a terrible nausea, a coated tongue, and the inability to regulate his temperature. He wanted to wrap himself up in the blanket, but at the same time he was covered in a patina of sweat. The Arizona June was in full effect. He tried to keep his movement minimal until his nausea was under control. As he came to a sitting position, he kept his head down and studied the black dress pants. These were the same pants that he wore day in and day out and what others had come to regard as not really dress pants at all. Through the years he had learned that immersing himself into an object eased his mind, and he tried it now. He stared at the fabric until the single threads became visible. He could make out the weave of fabric much like pores on skin, thin gray lines on black. He then turned his head as slowly as his nausea would allow and studied the small adobe room, looking at what he had seen every day for seven months. Its small size seemed to trap the heat. Likewise, its small size caused a momentary panic, a sensation of confinement, which quickly subsided. It was a moment of dread not unlike the Bad Thought, and he gently, with little movement, pulled the blanket from his lap. He wanted to be outside as soon as he was physically able.

"Ah, Señor Brody, you are not asleep." It was Old Mariana, bringing in a fresh bowl of water. "I have water for your head, yes?"

"Oh, hell, Mariana," he said, coming to his feet. "What does jacal mean in Mexican? Adobe shithouse?" He attempted to speak through a motionless mouth.

"Do not say those bad words, please. I put some water on your head and some water on floor, and we make the dust go."

Looking again at the ten-by-twelve-foot hovel, Edwin Brody nodded his head but did not speak. He had been this sick so many times that he knew speaking would only agitate his condition, although he no longer feared vomiting. He knew the routine: he would put a cold rag on his head, alternate sweats and chills, then run to the door to throw up in the dirty street. He could never make it to the outhouse in time, and if he went now, when he was able, he would just have to kneel on the dirty outhouse floor until the purging came. And any food would have to wait until later or maybe even the next day, unless he purged early. There was no point in trying to eat anything until after that event.

Holding the cool rag to his forehead, he forced himself to the doorway. Looking to his left, the south, silhouetted by the darker purple mountains behind it, he could see the rest of the village, which in any bigger town than Fuerte Viejo would have been called Mexican Town or La Zona Mexicana. There were some thirty or forty small jacals like his, tan in color and not much bigger than some cell in an eastern prison. They were scattered and in no sign of order, as if they had been flung down from the hand of a giant. There was also La Cantina, a much larger building of two rooms, which was of the same adobe but painted white, with a yellow sun painted over a once bright but now faded blue sea. He had spent most of the night there. And behind his own squalid hut, out of sight from the doorway, Brody knew there was the firm presence of the old destroyed mission fort that gave the town its name. Simply a chapel and the remnants of thick walls that were mostly crumbled masses on the desert floor, it was nonetheless always there, casting a very small sense of conscience and dread over him.

Across the absurdly wide street was the two-story saloon unsuitably named the Nantucket Whaler, and farther north, to his right, were the stores and homes that made up the Anglo town, Fuerte Viejo proper. This was the home of the miners and prospectors and the four or five wives who had come west with them. Still mostly adobe, though with some sunbaked wood and more color, it looked as ancient as a biblical town, and it was all tainted with the direct and heavy hand of Farrell O'Meara, the biggest man in a small, small town. There were other businesses and saloons farther up, not in his line of vision, but the pall of O'Meara would be present there too.

This was the home of the 140 or so men and women who made up the small town of Fuerte Viejo and who searched for mineral ore and farmed its fields to the north, south, and west.

CHAPTER 3

FRIDAY MORNING

Bendix hustled down the interior wooden stairs of the Nantucket Whaler and walked quickly though the saloon. O'Meara was in no good mood and had given him his first chore of the day. Sooner or later the old drunk would be having him hold his pecker while he peed. But O'Meara had the power, and next to him, feeding on the spillage, was where Bendix wanted to be. Nobody was in the Nantucket Whaler but Billy the bartender, because hell, even in a boring little town like this, everybody had something to do besides drink at 10:00 a.m. This week almost every white man was out in the desert picking rock and kicking gravel, trying to find some mythical lode that probably had already been found by a Spaniard centuries earlier, if it had ever even existed at all. But giving Billy a job like wiping down a counter for fourteen hours at a time kept him from getting into trouble.

Bendix found the little Wheeler kid sitting on the front step and gave a quick whistle. "Hey, you, don't ya got better sense to be seen outside a saloon at your age? And go get Brody and tell him Mr. O'Meara wants him here fast. Move!"

From where he stood in his doorway Brody heard nothing but the word "move," but he knew what was about to happen. Last night, after he'd buffaloed the Mexican stranger, he had mouthed off about telling O'Meara to go to hell. He had bitten that old drunk bastard's hand, so to speak, the one that fed him, and now he was going to get his talking to. He watched the Wheeler kid amble over slowly and saw Bendix grab an empty beer or soda bottle off the porch's bench and throw it at the kid's rear.

That's like him, he thought, without really being cognizant of the individual words. *The smaller the victim, the bigger the Bendix.*

"Well, Mariana," he said, still holding the rag. "It looks like I've got a meeting with the boss. What should I tell him? That I quit?"

"You stay here for the *gente,* the people. The people need you. You are not the bad man you think you are."

Before he could answer Mariana, the Wheeler kid was there, and before the kid could relay the message, Brody told him, "I know."

Then he turned to the peg on the door and grabbed his holster and the Remington Army. Just as he finished the buckle, he wretched, bending well forward so as to not splatter his boots and black dress pants. He knew he sounded like a tortured animal as he screamed out his purges. He was clearly violating Victorian dignity and mores, but this far west, morals were quite relaxed. It continued for several minutes, and he almost collapsed in it. Mariana handed him another cool, wet towel, and he draped it over his head, thinking he must look like the boxer resting between rounds at the match he had seen in New Orleans. He gave a final wipe of his entire face and tossed the rag back onto his sweat-stained sheets.

"Well, today just may be the day." He took a swig of cinnamon water and swished it around his mouth before spitting it onto the dirt floor. Collecting himself, he turned into the street and headed toward the Nantucket Whaler Saloon and O'Meara's office on the second story. As he walked with a sideways canter, he turned his head toward the mountains. The barest top of the chapel was

visible behind his hut, and it caused him to hitch his step as he noticed it. He tried to ignore it and instead focused on the rich colors
of the purple, saguaro-studded mountains and their deeper shadows beyond the chapel. It made him feel more relaxed. Despite the
haze in his head and the emptiness in his stomach, the sight made
him feel good.

CHAPTER 4
FRIDAY MORNING

Lieutenant Emilio Barzaga clasped his hands in nervous energy and stared at the dispatch on his desk. Anxiously, he anticipated its message. Was it directions to strike against the rancherias of the Apaches, or to pursue the marauding Hombres? He hoped neither. The Apaches had begun the spring with an outburst of violence, especially in the area of Fronteras.

Don Fernando de la Hoya had lost two vaqueros and close to twenty horses during the last week of March. Three mule drivers had been discovered stretched out on the desert floor, where they had been tied and set afire. Second- and third-hand information had indicated that their arms and legs had been slashed and that their genitals had been removed. He had heard of two children being stolen from a small village, and there were probably other victims whose disappearance had not yet been relayed to him. Perhaps now they were raiding Chihuahua, or up among the *norte americanos*. That was fine with him. Let them hit the fat Americans; they had more to steal and would feel it less.

Los Hombres too had been quiet for some months. This collection of army deserters and bandits robbed villages in Sonora and Chihuahua and stagecoaches and banks in Arizona and New Mexico. It was Lieutenant Barzaga's conclusion that they resided in a big city such as Fronteras, Juarez, or El Paso. That way, he reasoned, they could blend with the populace and not have to worry about defending a single small village or hideout. They, like the Apaches, were not averse to traveling scores of miles to find prey or to elude pursuers. To Barzaga, one directive would be as bad as the other. It was clear: whomever the enemy, kill them all, because they would not accept surrender from any Mexican soldier. Win the battle, die in combat or by your own hand, for the alternative was to be staked to the hard desert floor or tied to a saguaro for a lingering death.

He resigned himself to open the letter and smiled more broadly as he read each line. Captain Luis Alvarez, his distant cousin, was directing him to lead a detachment of twelve mounted troops and proceed north to Tumulca on the international boundary. At Tumulca they were to secure a wagon that would be waiting for them. The order read further that the wagon was to be escorted to Fronteras. Alvarez was giving him five days, three north and two south, which would allow Barzaga and his men to swing farther to the west and travel more safely. Traveling in that direction would keep them out of the dangerous lairs of the Apaches in the Sierra Madres. It would have to be done with as much speed as these sorry troops could muster, but it was possible. "Ah, good cousin," he sighed.

This was an opportunity to instill some discipline into his men and for them to prove their soldierly ability. This was a chance to fight back against the boredom that was the great disease of the entire Mexican army. This was a chance to clear that pestilence of desertion that plagued all of the army of Mexico in general and his unit in particular. "Yes, good cousin. It will be done."

CHAPTER 5

FRIDAY MORNING

Peter Heydt sat on the old wooden bench in front of the express office. It would be slow again today because the stage only came to Fuerte Viejo instead of Santa Ynez if there was Apache trouble, or if there was paying fare going south to Tumulca. As always, and especially after last night's ruckus at La Cantina when Edwin Brody had arrested that Mexican, he kept the Henry rifle next to him. Life was slow but punctuated with sudden bursts of excitement, and when danger did come, he wanted to be prepared.

Spying Brody sauntering across the street, he said in an even tone to Old Micah, the storekeeper, "Looks like another town meeting."

Old Micah gave his broom a rest on his elevated storefront, but only for a second, long enough to give a loathsome look at the town drunk—or town constable, depending on the time of day. "Well, it's about time that Mr. High-and-Mighty got himself told. And it's about time the teller got told too!" He gave a chuckle. The old Yankee storekeeper was always tickling himself. He thought he had the kind of sophisticated humor that these California rubes and eastern castoffs just did not understand. There was no love on his part for Brody or O'Meara. There was only one real mercantile store in town, his, but to get supplies, he had to pay the Haslett Brothers Express Company (of which Heydt was agent) a pretty penny. Or he could contract one of O'Meara's teams and hope the Hombres did not pirate it. O'Meara's teams were not cheap, not by a long shot, but they were slightly less costly, and they could be hired on shorter notice than Heydt's. He had thought O'Meara would have treated him better. Certainly he had expected O'Meara to treat him more respectfully. Damn one and damn the other.

Old Micah took another quick look but never let his sweeping stop. "Yep, I'd like to be a fly on the wall of that hotel. Yes, sir!"

Heydt, a tall and lanky Wisconsin Swede, was not as sure. O'Meara was a true bastard and owned a piece of just about everything in town: the hotel, the Nantucket Whaler, the liquor delivery, freighting, the Mexicans and Papagos who could hammer wood and make adobe, and even the fields themselves. It was his town, and aside from keeping a business across the street from the hotel, Heydt did not deign to come close to the old pickled boss, or jefe, as the Mexicans called him. And although he liked Brody, and had drunk liquor and played cards with him, he was not a friend. That man was fighting some kind of inner demon. Or conscience, he guessed, would be a better turn of phrase. O'Meara could tell Bendix to jump and it would happen. O'Meara would tell Brody to jump and Brody would do it, but with a good deal of reluctance, or maybe not at all. Brody's self-hatred and his hatred of the boss, the town, and the whole damned world would one day explode. Peter Heydt hoped that when that day came, he would be away in Santa Ynez or holed up in his office with the Henry rifle and a hell of a lot of cartridges.

CHAPTER 6
FRIDAY MORNING

Brody sauntered past Billy the barkeep and started up the narrow staircase that would take him to Farrell O'Meara. Bendix stood at the top, looking arrogant. "Hurry up, the boss is waiting."

"You'd do well to keep that smart mouth of yours shut, Bendix. I'm not really in the mood for you, and since you're already scared…" He turned on the landing and looked Bendix in the eye, moving close until their noses almost touched. "Just know that it won't take but one wrong word to get your fat ass in the ground."

"You can't talk to me like that! This is my saloon!"

"It ain't your nothing. It and you belong to that old man behind the door. Now open that door, and keep your fat ass out of my way."

When the door opened, it was plain that the "old man" had heard everything. He was sitting at his desk with no vest and no coat, adopting less formal attire for business that would not have been suitable back east. His face was bloated and red, the sure signs of alcohol at work on his heavy frame. His long hair flew away from his head, which was also an indication that he had been running his fingers through it all morning. Was he worried about business, Brody, or maybe that arrested Mexican?

"Go ahead and sit down, you. We need to talk." He studied his subject and reached into his right desk drawer to retrieve a pad of paper. "I brought you here about what, seven or eight months ago, is that right?"

Brody nodded his head. The damned old rascal knew it was seven months, probably even knew how many hours and minutes had passed since he'd first come to this hot and dusty cauldron that served as their village.

"Yes. That's about right, I think," O'Meara said. "It was seven months ago when I heard about that saloon incident in Texas—er, El Paso—and I said to myself, 'Farrell, there is a young man who can handle himself.' I thought we could bring you here, see, give you a nice room and meals, and you would keep this town in good order as the constable. But that hasn't happened, has it?" His keen eyes bored a hole in Brody's chest. Apparently he did not have the guts to look his subject in the eye, like a man. Bendix stood against the wall with a smug grin.

"Last night there was a ruckus over in that Mexican saloon. You got really into a bottle, as they say, and some poor old vaquero got his head knocked in. That's bad, see. See, that makes the papers in Santa Ynez and Prescott and then on to San Francisco and Saint Louis. People read about the town constable getting drunk and banging heads and they don't want to come here. See, people read that and they want to go somewhere else, maybe to the Gila or the Salt or maybe even Mesilla. Now you don't want that, do you?"

Bendix broke in. "He don't care, Mr. O'Meara. He don't care about anybody but himself."

Brody stood up as if to leave, then pulled the Remington from its holster and held it at arm's length, aimed at Bendix. "Just say the word and you'll have one less man on your payroll."

O'Meara rose slightly. "See, see, that's what I mean! This is un-acceptable! We can't have this. Bendix, get out of here, leave now. Dammit, Bendix, go!"

"Not yet he ain't leaving," said Brody in what was almost a whis-per. He felt a terrible chill, and there was a hollowness in his frame that was more than just the morning's purging. Slowly, almost without noticing, he began to lift one foot slightly off the floor, just the heel, then replaced it and lifted the other. In a moment he was rocking back and forth with the smallest of motions. His empty left hand clenched and released repeatedly. A distant noise like the rushing of far-off river rapids began in his ears. "That son of a bitch isn't leaving here armed to shoot me in the back. Whatever you got, drop it." But the roar was so loud he never heard his own words until the last one, which seemed so loud that it echoed in the wooden chamber. The long black barrel wavered from his physical weakness and from his bursting emotion. He began blinking rapidly.

Bendix looked as if he knew these might be his last few moments. He was not sweating with fear but looked like the only man in all of the territory, besides Brody himself, who was clammy and cold. He shook his head slightly, signifying no, but with no great amount of movement that would send his adversary the wrong idea. He pictured the roar and tongue of flame at any moment.

The pistol cocked. "I won't say it again. Oh my God, I won't say it, not once more. Throw down your piece." Brody was getting wild-eyed and continued his gentle, barely perceptible marching in place. Clearly, he was becoming manic.

This time Bendix reached down ever so slowly with his right hand and pulled a Wells Fargo model from his trouser pocket. He let it drop to the floor with a loud thud that belied its small size. It too even seemed to echo in the quietness of the hotel room. Bendix winced when it landed as if he thought the sound had come from Brody's Remington. He released a raucous fart, then raced from the room and clambered down the steps, presumably to the outhouse.

The wild-eyed man now turned his gaze to O'Meara, who was standing behind the desk. He suddenly realized that his gun was at arm's length and cocked. He shook his head as if to clear his gaze and let the hammer fall gently. After holstering it, he placed both hands over his face and let out a loud sigh. He was scared of what had just transpired. He did not want to kill another man, not after what had happened in El Paso. He couldn't stand it. Later he would have to go to bed and ponder his position and why he continued to fall into these moments of tension and drama and danger and remorse.

"I protect your interests, Mr. O'Meara, or at least I'm supposed to. That greaser in the jail is not a vaquero, or a freighter, or the goddamned king of Spain." He sat but continued to speak through the hands that covered his face. "Maybe I was drunk or acting out, you know, like I wasn't supposed to, but he is one of the Hombres. Not one Mexican in town has ever seen him, yet he was real familiar about the layout here."

He removed his hands and looked at O'Meara with an intense expression. "He knew what was planted where, even though nothing is really green or even hardly out of the ground yet." He paused, feeling like this much energy was going to make him vomit again. "And he had a lot of money, a lot. Well, anyway, he got wordy and I popped him. And when I get a meal in me and feel better, I'm going down there and find out who he is and what those damned Hombres are up to. Sweating in that hot jail all day will take some of the steam out of his boiler."

O'Meara looked exasperated and shook his head. "We are going to release that young man right now, see," he said, stabbing his desk emphatically with a short, thick finger. "When the Hombres come again and raid those fields"—he indicated the orderly rows out the window behind him—"then we will fight them and give them what for. But locking up someone we don't know is only going to attract the US marshal, or maybe even the Mexican authorities. We're close enough to the border to have real trouble. Maybe the governor of Sonora sends a little detachment up here, see. No sir, that vaquero gets out right now."

"Now." He reached into his pocket and pulled out a two-dollar coin. "If you want to stay here and eat my free meals and drink my free beer, then you will do what I say. Maybe I need to tell Billy that you're taking a rest from beer for a while. And I'll tell DeGarza at the cantina that you can't take anything stronger than water and beans. You look like you could get some strength up. Go tell Billy to have Abraham fix you a steak and some eggs, and we will talk again this afternoon. See to that now."

Brody clutched his stomach and headed for the door. He felt bad now, as bad as when he had first awakened. He was at the door when O'Meara made one final statement. "I mean it. He gets out today." Brody was grateful that if old O'Meara had heard about the things Brody had said after the arrest, he made no mention of them now.

CHAPTER 7

FRIDAY MORNING

Once O'Meara could no longer hear the thud of Brody's boots hitting the stairs, he stood and paced the small room. Crossing his arms and resting his forehead against the window pane, he stared thoughtfully out at the fields spreading toward the west and the immense stand of saguaros behind them. Eventually his gaze settled onto his inner thoughts, seeing nothing that lay before him. He reflected on the events that had brought him here. Last year, in San Francisco's Barbary Coast, a citizen from Mesilla had approached him with hopes of gaining some capital to secure the mineral deposits presumed to be around Fuerte Viejo. Wisely, or so he thought, he bypassed the plea and went straight to Santa Ynez and then Fuerte Viejo himself. His plan would skip any reckless mining ventures and rather follow the maxim that there was always money in mining the miners. After securing the lots of the almost abandoned town, he had placed a couple of articles in the San Francisco *Chronicle* and the Arizona *Miner* that hinted at lost treasures and lodes of gold, silver, and copper. The miners had come, but unfortunately the lack of any bonanza had stymied growth. Small dividends here and there did not amount to enough to garner a mine. If something were not found soon, there would more people leaving than arriving in town. And now, to top it all off, Brody was getting unmanageable. Seven months ago O'Meara had thought he was hiring a mean man who could handle a gun and be kept quiet with money. Instead he had gotten a damned unreconstructed lunatic that would be locked in an institution were they anywhere but in Arizona. Damn that impudent little drunk. Damn him and all the southern trash who were unwilling to cede their damned codes of honor and their damned sense of individuality. *He* had found this wretched little town, *he* had made the needed improvements, *he* brought in the capital and lured the prospectors. They all owed him. Why did they not see it? If he did not act soon, his dreams of prosperity would go to ruin.

Returning to his desk, he scribbled out a quick note on a sheet of fine writing paper. This was business. It was not what he had wanted, but progress, his progress, could not be held up by the likes of one crazed and deranged man. Once the handwritten note was placed in a bottle, he would have Bendix take it south of town to a certain rock ledge that was marked by a pronounced giant cactus. There his business partners would have their instructions. That much had been planned for weeks. Then he would have Bendix ride back north and over to Santa Ynez. This plan was new and unfortunately spur of the moment. He did not like that. But Brody was no longer an asset. He held little doubt that the lawman had to be removed. Now was the time for Bendix to find Greybib Calhoun. Not a pretty thought, but necessary. Yes, Greybib would take care of this mess. O'Meara just hoped the cure would not be worse than the ailment.

CHAPTER 8
FRIDAY MORNING

The Apache Indian alternated his movements, raising the eyeglass to see the town and then lowering it to study the area with his naked eye. Walking Knife was in a very dangerous position, sandwiched on the mountains between the towns he knew as Santnez and the smaller Fairty Bayho. But he was confident in his stealth, ability, and maybe, if such a thing even existed, his luck.

"Walking Knife," whispered his Mescalero friend, Red Buffalo Calf, "you are going to get us killed. I was a fool to travel so far from home so that my bones can fertilize the fields of the Papagos."

"Be quiet, my friend. We should be in great danger trapped between two villages so close together. But the whites and Mexicans are lazy and would rather ride a horse in a big circle than walk the mountains that separate them. If we wait until the sun is fully overhead and the town below is napping, we can walk straight north and camp outside the Place of the Two Strange Men. From there we can go to the Arivaipas or the Pinals, or we can go home. You may be afraid like a young boy, but look at what you have seen. No Mescalero has come this far west. The People should know all of the land that is theirs."

Although he was not known to any white man, and was but twenty years old, Walking Knife was already known among the natives of Apacheria. He was a Mimbreno of the Red Paint People, from the area north of the Pinos Altos mines, but even among a wandering tribe he was a traveler, a man who had seen more than most. His tribe loved land, not for ownership but for the materials of life that the land gave. There were saguaro flowers for ceremony and prickly-pear pads to heal wounds. There were ocotillos to form the framework of wickiups. There were buffalo to the east who gave meat and hide, and there were Pimas and Papagos to the west who provided crops for stealing. To the north were the Zunis and Moquis for blankets and silver, and for others than himself, there were Mexicans in the south to supply horses, guns, and women. But Walking Knife would never go south again.

Though the tribe loved its land for what it could provide, Walking Knife, who was also known as Big Eyes because of all that he had seen, loved the land for itself and for its mysteries. He had been to Ojo Caliente too many times to count to experience its warm waters. He had been on the plains of the Mescaleros to hunt buffalo. He had raided Mesilla with his Chiricahua cousins as a young man, and then Santnez (Santa Ynez) as an adult, secreting his stolen blankets and a couple of rifles in the beautiful Chiricahua Mountains. He had a secret cache in the Florida Mountains as well. He had seen the empty cliffside village of the ancient ones at Gila many times, and lost many nights' sleep waiting to see if ghosts would really appear there. He had been among the Arivaipa (Black Rock People), the Pinals, the Coyoteros, and even once, when he was in a camp of Tontos (the Hard to Understand People), he had met the strange Yavapais, who spoke neither Apache nor Mexican. Among his own band he was Walking Knife, named for the peculiar and beautiful Mexican knife he carried, or sometimes Big Eyes because of all that he had seen. But among the other bands, he was called Always Visitor, No Home Man, and Strong Feet. These names were all based on his desire and ability to see all of Apacheria, except for Old Mexico. They were also based on the fact that Walking Knife, like all Apaches, was not allowed to say his own name, even when visiting.

Walking Knife had no vision to tell him to travel, just a strong urge and curiosity. He would someday visit the end of the earth where all land stopped, or so the Yavapai had told him through the Tontos. But he would never go to Mexico, not even on a raid, because that was no longer Apache land. That land no longer belonged to the People. The Janeros and the wild men of Juh may live there, and his fellow Mimbreno Geronimo had married and resided there, but only by necessity. He thought those bands and such men had given up their birthright to live in a hostile land just so they could steal more easily, and to stay close to missions and drink liquor and in turn get their heads bashed in, or to trade for pinole that would be poisoned. He had heard enough and did not want to go to a land that drank so much Apache blood. He had been there before and found that the land gave him a bad feeling. He could feel that the air and ground were different. Mesilla, Pinos Altos, Santnez, and the scattered ranches of Sonoita had just as much worth stealing, and they were on land that was already Apache. All up and down the Rio Bravo were ranches full of tasty mules and less desirable cattle. Let the Mexicans have Mexico. Its land was dirty with too much Apache blood.

No other Apache thought him foolish for his wandering, nor did any think him a coward for his refusal to go to Mexico, for a man told himself what to do. And he was no coward or campfire woman, because he had proven himself in battle with miners, ranchers, and wagoners many times. They thought his spirit told him what to do and what his magic was and that was that. Maybe the great Ussen instructed him to wander so. But Walking Knife did not believe in spirits, ghosts, or even Ussen. He did not believe in anything.

CHAPTER 9
FRIDAY MORNING

Peter Heydt was still sitting on his front bench and starting to feel the weight of the morning sun when he saw the town constable walking toward him. He looked to his left to see Old Micah's heel as it flashed into the store's doorway. Old Micah was ornery, but he was also very afraid of saying the wrong thing, pissing off Brody, and winding up rotting under a pile of stones two thousand miles from Boston. To his right he saw Spencer (sometimes called Two Spencers because that was his name and because he carried a seven-shot Spencer on his saddle) coming toward him, and it looked like both parties were going to get to him at the same time.

"Well, goddamn, Spencer," said Brody in an unintendedly mean manner, "if I had anything besides these black pants, I'd tell you that you don't wear anything but the same brown vest and the same brown shirt and the same brown hat every day. You think we'll ever get tired of looking like we do?" It was meant to be humorous, but the tone was too flat. The cursing was uncalled for, uncharacteristic, and so was ignored. He was also pawing at his pant legs and fidgeting his hands, sure signs that he was dangerously anxious. Brody was trying to make them believe that he felt fine.

Spencer smiled. "Big Edwin Brody. How is my friend the Georgia goober? You know that's what we called Georgia soldiers we saw in the war—goobers. We could call y'all names, but we could never call you cowards. You boys never ran." It was too soon to talk about the war, and good manners dictated that nobody ever mentioned being on one side or the other. Arizona had too many holdovers from the California Column and too many Texas youths running from Reconstruction. And there were men from farther east who just wanted to be in a new place that did not remind them of the horrors they had seen. But Spencer was a good man and never said anything that one could consider meanspirited. His remark was in bad taste and impolite, but not meant to be offensive.

"I've a steak and some eggs on order at the hotel. Y'all had breakfast?" asked Brody. He saw the inquisitive faces of Heydt and Spencer and continued as if to answer their unasked question. "I feel well enough to eat. For right now, anyhow."

"Yeah, I had breakfast about four hours ago, but I'll go and watch you eat," said Spencer. The Spencer rifle was off the saddle and in his hands. He slapped it gently against his pants as he spoke. "Guys, I've got some odd news. Yesterday I was bringing some cornmeal back from the Maricopa Tanks and hailed in front of the McCord brothers' ranch. You know, the one at the fork of the north-south road?" As if the one house on the only road north were unknown to them. "They said a stage had gone by and stopped there for water, and the driver said that after he emptied in Santa Ynez, he would double back and be swinging around to Fuerte Viejo today to drop off two passengers. We're gonna have ourselves a growing populace here in Fuerte Viejo."

"Growth like that and we'll have our own territory cut from Arizona." Heydt laughed. "Hey, Spence. You said you talked to the McCords, but I bet you didn't. You might have spoken with Lucas, but I'll wager that spooky old Matt just stayed in the house. Spooky old fellow probably had a rifle on you the whole time and you didn't know it."

Edwin Brody shook his head and sat down on the bench. "Heydt is right. That is a fact. Those are the two unfriendliest men ever.

You'd think living on the edge of nowhere they would be dying for some company. Spencer, did Lucas McCord even ask you to light off your wagon? I stopped by there some months ago looking for signs of Hombres and asked for some water. Lucas, or whichever one has a beard, acted like I was asking for biscuits, honey, and butter. I finally just told him he could keep his damned water."

Before Spencer could reply, Brody looked away and retreated into himself. He could do it that quickly. Mentioning the water had reminded him of the Mexican still cooped up in the jail. While the other two droned on, apparently without perceiving that he was no longer listening, he turned his thought to that vaquero still locked away. Why was he here, and where had his money come from? Then there was Bendix. That Yankee bastard had been scared and embarrassed, and would be sore for some time. What might he do about it? Edwin did not think that Bendix had the bravery to kill a man, but then sometimes killing was the cowardly way out. Maybe knowing about his own Texas saloon incident would keep Bendix from doing anything. Brody had to admit that whether people knew the full story, or if they even believed it, it got him a lot more respect than he deserved. It was enough to keep him alive and fed by O'Meara. He was starting to feel ill again, and strangely naked. It was if merely being out in front of the Haslett Express office was akin to being on an acting stage, with all eyes on him. He wanted to curl up and hide.

Soon Spencer broke off a sentence and looked north through town. There was the barest dust cloud from running horses. The stage from Santa Ynez had left early and was already close. The road wound some and did not make a direct approach. There were two arroyos to cross, so it would still be some time before its arrival. Brody stood up, and it was evident to his companions that he had been trying to feel fine a moment ago and was now almost sick again. It came and went every minute. "Come on, Spence, Heydt, join me in the saloon."

CHAPTER 10

FRIDAY MORNING

Slack-jawed Billy the barkeep placed a smoking steak and eggs down in front of Brody and ambled back behind the bar. He did not do the cooking himself. That was the job of Old Abraham, who had a cookhouse to the side of the hotel. Heydt sat beside Brody so that they both would face the bar and thereby get a good look at any disembarking passengers, because the stage always pulled up to the front of the Nantucket Whaler. Spencer stood at the end of the bar, nosy enough to want to get the closest look and strike up a conversation. His carbine lay on the bar in front of him.

The saloon door swung open, and a tall, thin man with a weathered complexion and dressed entirely in black walked to the bar and stood in front of Billy. "I'll have some strong tea there, fellow, or if you'll tell me where in town I can get some...?"

"We have St. Louis and Milwaukee beers and liquor. Tea will be extra."

"Well, I can—" Suddenly the stranger broke off as he really looked at Billy for the first time. Billy had been kicked in the head by a horse, and his misshapen skull and misplaced eye told anyone that the brain beneath could not be fully functioning. His slack jaw and vacant stare cast off any lingering doubts. "Well," he started again. "I can pay the extra. What is your name there, fella?"

"Billy. Billy the barkeep. I'm the barkeep here. I tend bar."

"Okay, Billy, thanks." He turned around to study the inside of the Nantucket Whaler and to close off any further discussion with Billy, who finally got motivated to shuffle out the side door and over to Old Abraham's.

"Don't mind Billy," said Spencer. "He just does the best he can, and we make allowance for it."

"Thanks, friend. Don't like speaking ill of a young man like that, but I guess you keep your expectations low and he can meet 'em. Thanks for letting me know."

Billy returned at that time with a large coffeepot and a pewter mug. "Lucky Old Abraham drinks tea too, or else you'da had to drink coffee. He's a colored man."

The stranger let out a slow "yeah" as if he was not sure how to follow that line of reasoning.

"We don't get many people coming to Fuerte Viejo, mister," said Billy. "What kind of work you gonna do? You gonna mine?" His mouth hung open as he waited for a reply.

If the stranger were offended by the rudeness, he didn't let on. "Well, Billy, my name is McLeroy Banks. I have tanned leather, worked as a freighter and a wheelwright, tended a farm, driven a stage, and even done some blacksmithing and soldiering. But one thing I will never do is chop cotton."

"Are you too good to chop cotton, sir?" Spencer asked, his grin showing he meant no offense.

"Why, no, I'm not," laughed Banks. "And therein lies the rub." He held up his brown and calloused hands to show that they had seen plenty of work, presumably on southern cotton fields. Heydt and even Brody chuckled.

Banks continued. "As of late I have been residing in Prescott, but since they won't let me live in the fort without enlisting, and since the local sons of Cain are keeping things too hot, I have decided to relocate to a healthier climate." Banks relayed this with a bit of feigned superiority that assured his listeners that it was said with some jest.

To everyone's surprise, Brody spoke next. "You're welcome to sit here with us, Mr. McLeroy Banks."

The newcomer obliged, bringing the pot and mug with him. Before anyone could speak next, a spectacled man came through the door carrying three carpetbags. "You find your tea here, Mr. Banks?"

"Yeah, and if you want any, you're welcome to some of mine." Banks raised his eyebrows at Heydt and Brody as if to ask if this were acceptable. "It'd be easier, trust me," he said under his breath, so that just his tablemates could hear. "Gentlemen, this is Professor Metz. He rode the stage from Prescott and made a long trip seem short. It seems he is here to study the locals. And I'm sorry, sirs, I don't yet know your names."

Sensing that his breakfast companion was feeling better (he always seemed to ebb and flow), Heydt welcomed them both with introductions, including Spencer, who joined them from his place at the bar. Edwin Brody took tiny bites, as if the smaller the bite, the lesser the effort and the greater his ability to keep it down.

CHAPTER 11
FRIDAY MORNING

"Professor Metz, it is a real pleasure to have a learned man in town. Are you a teacher professor or a studying professor?" queried Heydt.

"Well," answered the frail older man, peering over his spectacles, "I have taught at a number of colleges in New England, but I am making a large sojourn of this territory to ascertain the folklore, religions, medicines, and cultures of the aborigines. My benefactors and I are interested in whether these tribes are related, or if they are all individual and distinct. Thus far, from the Santa Fe pueblos, in which I have little interest, to the Navahos and Zunis, I have found little commonality. However, my benefactors feel that their long-term exposure to the Spanish colonial practices of this area make them of little value in a cultural study. The Yavapais or Yampis of Prescott made things 'too hot,' as you Westerners say, and I was forced here. Perhaps I can reach some of the Cherry Cow or Coyote Apaches, time permitting. Are there any reconstructed ones about?"

"You mean tame ones?" asked Brody. "Not hardly. You ride an hour out of town in any direction but west and you'll be graveyard dead."

"Well, I'd rather not use the term tame, if you please," replied Professor Metz. "I know I am a stranger in this land and not well versed in your sentiments and language, but I am a student of man, and I believe we are all brothers in Christ. I like the term 'reconstructed.' Since I'll be in town for a number of days, I think I should be forthright and tell you all that I was an abolitionist, and that in my learned opinion, we are all men, red, black, or white. I stand on these convictions, and I hope that it does not cause too much discomfort, as I am your guest."

"Lord, you talk pretty," said Spencer with a grin.

Heydt was very surprised that Edwin Brody let the rebuff pass without reply. "Professor," Spencer said, "this is a rough and wretched country you're in. Everybody in these parts was on one side of the war or the other. Back east, feelings are hard and both sides get real mouthy about the war. Out here there is a lot of meanness of feelings, but good manners prevent us from saying anything. Even I forget that some. But we here are all in the same boat, trying to make money and a living where there is little food, a lot less water, and a heck of a lot of angry Indians. There isn't a person in town who has not taken an Indian down or thrown a bullet at one, and plenty have lost a friend or a relation to them. I think everyone will be well pleased to have an educator among us. But nobody wears their sentiments on their sleeve here." He smiled to make his last sentence easier. "We're all in one sinking, godforsaken boat, and it's too small to make hard feelings."

"Oh my God!" Heydt grinned. "That was so pretty. Can I write that down?"

"Lord, Professor," laughed Brody. "It seems you have awakened the spirits of Stephen Douglas, Daniel Webster, and Abe Lincoln."

Spencer leaned back to cross his arms and legs. He blushed deeply. "Aw, why don't all of y'all just hush! You don't think I can read? I know big words and prose." He attempted to sound angry but had to stifle a giggle at the last word.

Heydt laughed. Actually, he had wanted to say the same thing, though ordinarily he did not see to other people's business. He hoped that the professor would heed the advice. And he was glad to see that Edwin Brody was in good humor with the conversation.

As Professor Metz laughed with them and shrugged, Brody pushed his plate away and told the newcomers of the pecking order of the town: the Mexicans generally stayed south of the Nantucket Whaler; the Anglos stayed mostly north but would go to Cantina; his hut was the dividing line; and if you wanted goods, there was Old Micah's or the day-long and dangerous trip to Santa Ynez. He also explained, with some unwanted assistance from Spencer, that the Apaches and Los Hombres kept things bottled up, that they stole but left just enough so the peasants did not pack up and leave for something better. He also informed the professor that he was the town constable, or marshal, and that though he could not scout the whole territory for hostile Apaches, he did intend to give the Mexican Hombres what for.

CHAPTER 12

FRIDAY NOON

While Spencer entertained Banks and Metz, Brody decided to excuse himself and take a walk. The Bad Thought had really worn him out yesterday, and already this morning he had reacted with such violence toward Bendix that it scared him. Sure, he would like to see Bendix dead; but to really do it, to take another man's life without serious enough provocation? He had been occupied in meeting the newcomers, but now his mind settled into its normal routine of self-inflicted torture. He felt that if he did not find something to occupy his mind, he would go insane. God, he hated himself.

The sun was high overhead when Brody exited the Nantucket Whaler. As a result, the western side of the mountains had run from their early morning purple to the midday red and brown. He studied the change momentarily before turning left and walking the wide empty street until he reached the last building in town—Harvill's Dress Shoppe.

Harvill's store was actually one-third of the largest structure in town. There was a small two-room addition of Nicks, the barber and undertaker. (Only two people had died in Fuerte Viejo in the past year, but numerous travelers on the road had been found pierced by arrows and tortured to death.) The middle or main body of the building was the Sam Houston Saloon. The final addition was Beverly's. Whereas the entire structure was of sand-scrubbed and sun-bleached wood, she had managed to find enough whitewash to make her end look respectable and even upscale. How she had managed to procure the fresh blue paint for the window trim was a mystery. She was truly the end of the road, for once past her, it was ten miles to the McCord brothers' ranch and another sixty to the Maricopa Tanks. A popular joke was that upon leaving hell, it was three days' ride through hell until you reached the Tanks, which were located on the outskirts of hell.

Brody counted to five, waited, then counted to five again before knocking and opening the door. It took a moment for his eyes to adjust to the dimmer light of the interior, but gradually he saw her sitting in a chair in the middle of the room. She sat with her skirt pulled up immodestly to her knees, and a small cigarette dangled from her pretty mouth.

"Please excuse me, Mr. Constable," she said as she quickly stood to let the hem of her dress fall. "Arizona is kind of hard on the women. Are you going to arrest me for such behavior?" She laughed as the words came out. She was not embarrassed by the brief glimpse of calf, but Brody clearly was.

He fumbled with his hands, then remembered to remove his hat. "No, Miss Harvill. Let's just say you get a suspended sentence." He was attempting to be funny but was obviously uncomfortable. His tone was flat and conversational, not at all humorous. With a raised eyebrow, he pointed to the chair beside her, and when she nodded, he took a seat.

"Well, Edwin Brody," she said, taking a bold puff of cigarette. "If it was any other man but you sitting here, he'd be talking a blue streak, trying to make me fall in love. You're shy, or something else. But before we touch on any subject, I do want you to call me Verly. I never want to hear you say Beverly or Miss Harvill." She smiled gently.

"Yeah, well." He grasped at his head and stared at the floor. "Shy or not, I've got something weighing on me. I know you're a good soul, Verly. Will you help me? I mean...will you try?"

She paused and gave a look of grave concern that he missed. She took another puff from her cigarette and rose to the door. She hung a CLOSED sign on the knob and locked it. "Some busybody or two will have something to say about us being in here together, but just let them talk. We can have our privacy." She paused to look for anyone on the street before she turned to face him.

Brody realized the implications of being alone and what she had said. "Good Lord, Verly! It never crossed my mind that being here would look that way. I'll leave. I'm so sorry."

He scrambled to collect himself, but she pushed him back down into his chair with a laugh. "I said let them talk, Edwin. For a rough-and-tumble frontier man, you sure are a nervous gentleman. But you're sweet, though. Thank you for thinking of me. It's very gallant. Now." She plopped down in an unladylike manner into her chair. "Please tell me how I can help you."

He took a moment to take in what he thought of as beautiful. She had curly blond hair and large, dark brown eyes with lashes so long and thick with paint that he guessed they could support weight. Her face too was heavy with what he thought was called rouge. It was probably considered distasteful. No Anglo woman in town or in Santa Ynez looked like Verly. If she was trying to hide behind such a painted facade, it was not working. Petite Verly Harvill was as open and true as a gaping window.

Before being considered rude, he returned his eyes to the floor. Seconds ticked by without him saying anything. He made several efforts to initiate the words, but he faltered. He wanted to tell her about the Bad Thought, but the words would not come forth. What would she think of him? Would she turn him away in derision?

"Edwin, I've always found the easiest way to unburden is to just say it. Say what is on your mind and be out with it." She grasped his arm with her hands. "Staying bottled up is the worst. Please tell me, Edwin. I'll help you if I can."

More seconds ticked by, and he made a deep guttural growl, an attempt to stifle a sob. Then he rose, shaking off her grip and hugging himself. "Aw, Lord, I'm going to pieces. Something is in me. Something is wrong with me."

She looked up in astonishment and some fear. This was no man looking for pity; this was a man about to hit bottom. Without true realization, Harvill became afraid for his safety and her own. Although fear covered her with an icy shroud, she was less aware of it than of her concern for him, which she found to be an almost physical ache. "Honey, please sit down."

He returned to the chair. She stomped out her cigarette and grasped his arm again with both hands. She gripped firmly enough to provide what she thought was assurance and comfort. With his face in his hands, hat discarded on the floor, he began again.

"Verly, please don't touch me. Don't even look at me. I can't have you see me like this." The tears were finally beginning to stream down his face.

"No, Mr. Constable." She gripped harder now. "You're doing fine, but you have to let it out. You have to let it out to feel better. I promise."

He sat back in the chair and covered his face with his left hand while she continued to hold onto his right. With great gasps, he fought back sobs. Through his fingers she could see him grimacing as if in the greatest pain. A foot in a bear trap could not have caused someone to look more hurt. "You'll not like me, Verly. I'm a bad person. I'm so bad."

"Was it those killings in Texas?" she asked in her most gentle tone. "In that bar? Honey, you're the only one thinks that bad. It was self-defense—"

"No!" he interrupted. "It goes back further than that. And that was just one killing, not three. Everybody wants to make more of it and it ain't so. But it goes back further."

"War killings, then? War killings ain't killings like regular ones. I know it's a burden to you young boys that had to face it. I've seen it myself."

"Aw, it wasn't any war killing, either," he said with what sounded a lot like annoyance. He wiped some tears away. "This is a terrible thing. You're so good and decent. Verly, you're so good."

Even more time elapsed as Brody struggled to compose himself. Verly Harvill took the opportunity to make and light another cigarette. She paced in front of her door with arms crossed.

"Edwin, I don't look down on nobody. Maybe you'd feel better if I told you some things about me." She picked up some lace in a basket and worked it with her fingers as she spoke.

CHAPTER 13

FRIDAY NOON

"My family moved from Tennessee to Missouri when I was real little," Verly said. "I barely remember it—the going west, I mean. After a while the war came. You'd have thought the need to feed soldiers would have made a farm successful. That wasn't what happened, though. There were so many problems with partisans and night riders and plain old thieving. Thieving was more common than anything else. We'd wake up and whole rows of corn would be cleared out. One night our drying house was cleaned out of every last scrap of tobacco. That was less to sell, and that meant less money to pay the bills on the farm. It also meant less money to buy supplies for the next season. I guess if you grew up on a farm you'd know."

Brody nodded.

"That was early on. Then one night some cavalry rode through and burned the drying house down. Another time it was the barn. All of our horses got confiscated by the Yankees, and then almost all our pigs by the Confederates. I remember they paid us in Confederate money, and Daddy just broke down and cried in front of us. We couldn't spend it nowhere. We finally took to keeping the chickens and young pigs in the house because there was just so much taking.

"Once the taxes got so high and we had no crops or bread or livestock and no way to pay for it, Pa lost it. I mean he lost it at the courthouse. When we returned to get our few belongings, some riders—I don't know which side and it doesn't matter—well, they rode by and shot him for not being a soldier. Mother and all us kids fled to St. Louis. There was work for women there. I was trained as a seamstress and learned a lot. But there was more money to be made by just being a girl young in her years. Do you understand me, Edwin?"

He grabbed her hand back. "Verly, you don't owe me this. I'm sorry; I truly am. Your struggle is so big and you're so strong. Please don't tell me any more."

She smiled thinly and grasped herself in a hug as he had done just minutes earlier. "No, Edwin." She turned to look at the door but was not seeing it. She was miles and years away. "No, Edwin, I'm not stronger or better than anyone else. We are just traveling different paths to the same destination. Anyway, turns out that as much as I enjoyed sewing, the money was better working at The House. It was beautiful. There was thick red carpet and fancy red chairs and sofas. There was red everywhere. And brass and mirrors! So shiny!"

Her eyes momentarily blazed with excitement before dying. "There was a lot of call for a girl my age. Most of the others were older or too fat from high living. Me? I was hungry and thin. My one rule was no darkies. But one night a free man came in and said he'd pay double just to have me. I said no, but Robert—he was the owner's husband and the force for the place—he said I'd do it or else. It turned into a struggle, and he dragged me out to the stable and whipped me with a buggy whip. He bound me to a stud and tore off my dress and tanned me to a fare-ye-well. I had to be with the darkie anyway, and Robert took all the money because he said I had been uppity."

He grasped her hand again. "Please don't, Verly. You don't owe me this!"

"No, honey, I don't owe it to you or anyone else. But I want you to know about me too.

"After that happened a kindly policeman who worked our area, dear sweet Gustav, he came to the House and worked Robert over good. He used his billy club on one cheek and then the other. I'm quite sure Robert lost a tooth or two. Gustav forced him to open the money box and give me five hundred dollars in gold coins. Well, I took off like a shot—like a scalded dog, as I've heard some people say. That was enough for me to set up in New Orleans. I made money there as those women will buy a dress when they don't have enough money to buy bread. But it was too tempting to go back to that other work. So I went to Houston, San Antonio, and then Santa Ynez to here. Each place made me more money than when I got there. But now I'm here, and this is as close to nowhere as I can get. Nowhere is where I belong."

"Verly." He looked her clearly in the eyes now. "You're like a beautiful flower. Each layer opens to show something new and just as beautiful."

"You're sweet, just like a little boy. Now you," she said flatly while wiping away one of her own tears. "You don't think any less of me? I mean, am I still worthy of your high esteem?"

He was slack-jawed in disbelief. "Well, yes! I mean…even more so. You're strong—strong like a man should be. Why on earth—no, *how* on earth can I think less of you? No." he shook his head. "No. You are everything."

She managed to smile for the first time since he had sat down in the shop. "That's nice, Mr. Brody. I think you mean that. But I've killed too." She nodded glumly. "I've killed, sure as the world. The very night I left St. Louis, my sister told me that dear sweet Gustav had been stabbed in the back. Killed. I know that was done on account of me and what Gustav had done to shame Robert. I can't change anything, though. I can lament it, but I can't change it. I have enough saved to finish my days unless something goes terribly wrong. There's dresses to make for the little Mexican girls' *quinceañeras* here and in Santa Ynez, and enough fine ladies in Santa Ynez who want my dresses for fiestas. If any white women—well, let me say if any *more* white women—move to Santa Ynez, they'll have to see me or else. Maybe I will move over the mountains and head east instead of always going west. I will make it, though. I'll do."

Brody stood as if to leave. His Bad Thought had been a torture since his childhood, but he saw for the first time in a long time, maybe since the war, that others suffered too. Others suffered hard lives, terrible guilt, and the anguish of the soul.

As if to break his reverie, from down the street came the pops of pistols and the heavier boom of old musket rifles. There were many of them. Without hesitation he flew to the door and flung it open, pistol in hand. "Stay here and lock the door behind me," he yelled as he raced over the wooden sidewalk and into the street. All around the jail, the air was clouded with powder smoke and dust, but through it all he could make out the tall sombreros of Mexican riders. Los Hombres! There was a long, loud thud, and even more dust arose from the back of the jail. All of the riders' activity centered around the one building. As the shots became more sporadic, he heard the thunder of hooves, and the great cloud moved west into the desert.

Breathless by the time he reached the Nantucket, he saw Spencer with his Spencer carbine in hand.

"You want to get some boys together and ride after 'em?" questioned Spencer.

"I'm in for it if need be," added Heydt.

"I am a citizen of Fuerte Viejo now and accept the societal obligation," said Banks. "Of course, I need loan of a rifle. I don't want to pursue with just handguns."

Despite his anger, frustration, and physically draining morning, Brody looked at Banks with good humor. "There is no need, gentlemen. We don't have enough for a proper posse, and I couldn't live with myself if anyone was to get hurt. Besides, they have fresh mounts not too far away. They probably rode their worst horses in and had the best ones staked out all fresh and ready for the final getaway. Let's all go home, people."

The few peasant farmers appeared unmoved, but only to the Anglos. In their hearts and minds, they knew this was bad. The law-man, Señor Edwin, would be in a bad way tonight. If Los Hombres came when he was sober, he would kill them all. Of that there was no doubt. But if they came again when he was drunk, when he would try to fight but would not be able to, then the whole village would be made to suffer.

CHAPTER 14

FRIDAY AFTERNOON

At the first shots, O'Meara raced to a window that looked down upon the jail. Through the smoke and dust he saw and heard a band of Mexican riders, all with pistols and long muskets. Several had lariats tied from their saddle pommels and thrown over the crossbeams of the jail. One other had his looped through the bars of the window, and all, with horses excited and straining, were pulling the back of the building free from the rest of the adobe edifice. It came down as one piece but cracked into many upon contact with the ground. Once the wall was over, they slashed the lariats free with absurdly large knives. Arkansas toothpicks, he thought they were called, or maybe machetes. Through it all the numerous riders shouted, hurrahing the town as it were, and firing their weapons into wood, glass, and air.

"Goddamn it all to hell!" O'Meara screamed. "They have no appreciation for who I am or for what I've done for this wretched place. Not those damned greasers and not that damned Edwin Brody. Why is it I say something and it doesn't happen?"

This was bad. The prisoner had now been released by other means. And Bendix had already left to place the message bottle south of town. In fact, it was so long ago, he was probably already back north of town and on his way to Santa Ynez.

"Goddamnit. Why does this always happen to me?"

43

CHAPTER 15
FRIDAY NIGHT/SATURDAY MORNING

It was well past moonrise by the time Bendix had rounded the long mountain and ridden into ancient Santa Ynez. He thought that on Friday night (though it was actually Saturday morning), the herdsmen from the small yet growing number of cattle ranches from close to the border would be filling up the hotels and boardinghouses. In fact, the cowboys, in conjunction with soldiers on leave from nearby Fort McKee and the usual merchants on return from Fort Whipple and the mines of that area far, far to the north, had swollen the town. Although the Cervantes House had empty rooms, he opted to rent half a bed with a snoring cowboy who had apparently reached his apex earlier in the day. This was evidenced not only by his loud breathing, but by the one boot he wore and the empty liquor bottle on the windowsill. It would be a long night for sure, but O'Meara had given Bendix coins for a single room, and now he could keep the difference.

Bendix had been told that Greybib Calhoun could most likely be found at the Lord Baltimore Saloon. He set that as his first course, walking the main avenue with the lights of the cantinas, saloons, and dance halls spilling into the street, providing enough

44

illumination to read a newspaper if one were so inclined. Plinking pianos or small ensemble bands, Mexican horns and guitars bled into one another. There had been continued building booms with each new rumor of a peace with the Apaches, but year after year the peace never came. Businessmen with capital moved in to explore mining, water, and cattle interests, and with them came more structures and the excitement of growth. But as harmony between the races never came to fruition, the town would settle back down until the next rumor arose. Even now the popular places of last year were almost vacant as centuries-old Santa Ynez, like most other western towns, strived to be more cosmopolitan and trendy to a population that had probably been living east of the Mississippi just months before. The town was still well over half Mexican, from the high-minded Flores and Lopez families to nameless masses like those in Fuerte Viejo. But again, as the rumor rose anew, the whites were growing in number and could count among their own the likes of the York family of Philadelphia. There was even talk of changing the name of Santa Ynez to something more sophisticated like Constitution, Lincolnburg, or even New Richmond or New Washington. It was really a matter of where one had spent the earlier part of the decade as to having an opinion on the latter two.

A quick glance inside the Lord Baltimore told Bendix that Calhoun was not present. The yellow walls and brass chandeliers and sconces cast as much light as at midday. The two faro tables flanking the front door were vacant. The three billiard tables captured the attention of just seven men. Three others, Hispanic businessmen or townsmen by their dress, occupied the bar. No tough customers here.

As he passed the St. Louis Beer Hall, a cowhand sailed out the door and into an unconscious heap on the dusty street. A monstrous bartender, well over two hundred pounds and wearing a white apron, stood brushing his hands as if to remove something filthy but unseen. "If anyone sees him trying to come back in here, you'd better stop him," he said to anyone within earshot.

The next saloon, the newest and most popular in town, was the Tahitian Palace. It was Santa Ynez's version of a South Seas paradise, and supposedly there was no place like it in Kansas, San Antonio, or San Francisco's fabled Barbary Coast. Bendix was all too glad to see its splendor before it got shot up and destroyed by drunken cowhands. "It won't last," he said to himself. "Santa Ynez has staying power, but this place don't." Once inside, he stepped to his right to avoid the push of customers going in and out.

Whereas most of the saloons and beer and dance halls had a multitude of candles and brass to brighten their interiors, the Tahitian Palace went to the opposite extreme. The numerous tables each featured a hurricane lamp of punched tin, and among them whirled fast-moving waiters, bilingual Mexican youths with eyes painted to make them look Chinese. Overhead and along the wall hung a multitude of paper lanterns of orange, yellow, pale blue, and purple. The effect seemed to provide more flickering shadows than actual light. In the far back corner, two hulking mestizos, supposedly friendly Polynesian natives, beat on large drums between two paper palm trees. Truly, there was nothing like the Tahitian Palace anywhere, and Bendix secretly and jealously wished that one of the glowing lanterns would spill over and turn the whole extravagant mess into a huge bonfire.

Over the din of drums, laughter, and loud conversation, he heard one voice. It seemed to carry more volume, like a drunken man who thought himself humorous. Bendix stood on his toes and glanced up and down the bar until he spotted the source. A large man, tall but not so big as he seemed, stood with his back to Bendix. He wore a filthy and battered gray hat. It was perched on the back of his head rather than on top, and it might have been held in place by the hardening agents of salt and sweat and dust. His gray shirt was stiff with the same three ingredients, plus a splash or two of beer. As Bendix approached, he was sure that he could smell him from five feet away. Two pistols of different size were tucked into his belt.

Working his way through the throng was tough, but Bendix made it to the bar and next to Calhoun. He waited impatiently while the herdsman related to his companions, also cowhands, a story about following the tracks of a lost cow into a box canyon of a range that Bendix had never heard of. That was not uncommon. Hills, creeks, mountains, and even entire ranges went by different names depending on which side of them the speaker lived on. Most maps were drawn and labeled by artists who had never seen what they were paid to convey. Even the range that separated the two towns was called the Purple Range or Santa Ynez Mountains on the Fuerte Viejo side, and the Big Indian Mountains or Viejo Mountains on the Santa Ynez side. Regardless, the entire conversation bored Bendix, and he guessed that the only thing worse than life in a town that refused to grow was raising cattle in a skillet-hot wilderness where towns were hard to come by.

CHAPTER 16
EARLY SATURDAY MORNING

B endix waited impatiently until Greybib finished his tale and the two companions wandered away. Then he tapped his quarry on the shoulder and gave a loud "Excuse me." Greybib finished his beer in a long gulp and wiped his mouth with his palm before giving Bendix his attention.

"Yes?" he said with something between humor and annoyance.

"My name is Bendix. I represent Farrell O'Meara over in Fuerte Viejo. He…" There was a moment's hesitation. "Uh, we would like to discuss a business transaction with you. A possible business deal."

Greybib looked the stranger up and down, trying to gauge the man's mettle. He was almost tall, but not as tall as himself. Also, Calhoun considered himself burly and intimidating, whereas this man was soft and pudgy. This Bendix was clearly more comfortable pushing dry goods or a pencil across paper, not working in the weather or soiling his hands. He wondered if the man had ever done any honest work in his life.

"I've heard of him. Why me?"

"O'Meara hires only the best." Bendix closed his eyes and gave a smug nod. "The best, like me."

Greybib's stomach turned. He had an almost overwhelming urge to put his meaty fist into this middle-aged dry-gooder's mouth. Nobody but a son of a bitch would come into a bar full of Texas drovers and declare himself "the best." Still, Calhoun had heard of Farrell O'Meara. If nothing else, the man had capital to throw around. He could not have gotten rich by surrounding himself with fools.

His curiosity getting the better of him. "What's this O'Meara got, a mine he wants protected? He want to acquire some cattle herds?"

Bendix continued with his aggravating smug expression. "No, nothing like that, Mr. Calhoun. Fuerte Viejo has a constable who has ceased to make himself useful. There is considerable coin in making him realize it."

Goddamn, thought Greybib. *Using the term "coin" like I'm some whore.* He clenched his fist again, trying to swallow the urge to knock this cur on his ass. "Let's grab a table and talk about it."

As he made his way to a table, those he pushed aside gave a quick glance back and then continued on their way. That did not escape Bendix's attention.

CHAPTER 17

SATURDAY NOON

Nuñez was not angry over being told to retrieve the message. He accepted the order with the knowledge that he had earned that perilous duty. It was he who had ridden into Fuerte Viejo. It was he who had gotten drunk and mouthy in La Cantina. And it was he who had endangered them all by getting his head knocked in by the gringo lawman. By getting thrown into the cheap little jail, he had placed all of Los Hombres in danger. Until he redeemed himself, he would ride drag on the herds of stolen cows and sheep and do the other shit jobs, like taking night watch on the trails. At some point, another member of the outlaw group would infuriate El Gato, and then *that* poor bastard would be low on the stick. Nuñez was grateful that El Gato had directed the men to brave the attack and have him released from jail. The gringo lawman had not given him food or water since placing him in the cell. Going without food was something he was accustomed to. In the harsh and unforgiving land of the Sonoran desert, food was a luxury. Water, however, was life itself. And though it had been a few brief hours from arrest to breakout, his thirst had driven him to panic and near madness. That gringo had not even been around for Nuñez to beg and plead for water. So in payment, Nuñez would do as he was told without bucking or making noise. He just hoped the next person to cross El Gato would do it soon.

Oh well, he thought. *Get the damned message. Be damned careful. And be damned quick.*

He was approximately two miles farther south than the southernmost jacal in Fuerte Viejo. Any closer and he would have been spotted by the poor farmers in their fields. Too much farther out and the protective cover of prickly pear, creosote, paloverde, saguaro, and mesquite would give way to the more fertile grassland, where riders were visible from miles away. To reduce his chance of exposure, he tied his horse to a paloverde tree some three hundred yards from the stagecoach road. It was a horse with no name, for it had had no name when Los Hombres stole it from the Pimas a week ago. It would never acquire a name. If and when the time came that he was in a lean way and had been without food, it would be tougher to eat something that had once been thought of in personal and affectionate terms. Only El Gato had a horse with a name: Midnight Sky. And El Gato would shoot one of his own men and eat *him* before he killed his beloved horse.

Nuñez worked his way through the Sonoran landscape. Across the road a moderately high hill could be seen, the first in a series of larger hills behind it. This promontory, one of the vestiges of the great mountain that separated Fuerte Viejo from Santa Ynez, was a tall formation of rock that dropped precipitously to a long shelf leading southward. It was studded with saguaros, but one in particular stood tall and almost symbolic, a titan among giants. It seemed as tall as a pine and had numerous arms, some of which themselves had arms. Nuñez had never been to school and had no inclination toward science, but he knew that this grand old dame of the desert was too old and too top-heavy to serve as a beacon for much longer.

Swiftly he moved over the road and up the gray-and-bone-colored incline until he was under the ledge of the shelf. There was

51

not room to stand, but a man could stoop or sit comfortably. This spot gave cover from rain and, at least for the first half of the day, from the oppressive sun. It was also an easy rifle shot to the rugged highway below. He was close enough to shoot accurately and above any possible prey. Also, if it was before noon, any adversary would have to look up into the sun to return fire. That was something to consider and put in his brain for later.

El Gato had instructed him to look for an old Indian carving in the wall, a spiral with a sun and a robed or square figure. What story they once conveyed no one knew. He had been told that the pictograph was faint, barely visible, yet he spied it from several feet away. Crawling on his hands and knees, Nuñez worked his way along the overhang. Yes, faded red designs were ascertainable in the gray wall. There they were. Though the whole shelf was of loose sand and shards of rock, almost like broken pottery or crockery but not, the patch here was of a looser mixture, indicating that it had been turned over recently. With much anticipation he pried his black nails through the soil. He went some inches easily. One more handful and a green vial of patent medicine exposed itself. From instinct he picked the bottle up and gave it a vigorous shake. Though nearly deaf due to years of gunfire and neglect of hygiene, he could detect a faint noise inside. There was also a delicate shift in weight. A quick glance at the road below told him he was still safe from any passerby. Therefore, without regard to injury, he smashed the bottle against a fist-sized stone.

Spreading the scroll on the ground, leaving dirty fingerprints as he did so, he scanned the paper for any words that he might know. Nuñez had never been to school. He had never learned more than a few words of English. The word "Tumulca" he could make out. The others were just squiggles of ink, as meaningless as if they had been done by a child. But one more word caught his attention, for it was longer than the others, and its first letter was larger. That was a sign of importance. He tried to sound it out; it was difficult because he did not recognize all the letters nor the sound associated with them. For several seconds he worked it over until it hit him like a splash of cold water. Yes! The script was different, but he was certain that he had seen it before on calendars in saloons and on advertisement in general stores.

"Good God!" he said to no one but himself. "This place—shit, all of Mexico and Arizona—is about to feel the fires of hell."

He scrambled down the slope much faster than he had ascended it and raced to his horse as fast as his cumbersome boots would allow. He considered riding away slowly to avoid a dust trail but said loudly, as if he had an audience, "Fuck it!" Then he reeled the pony westward to skirt Fuerte Viejo and get back to Los Hombres.

CHAPTER 18
EARLY SATURDAY AFTERNOON

McLeroy Banks exited the Nantucket Whaler, then turned to give it a cursory study. At one time it had been painted a dark nautical blue, but the sun and sand had worked the paint severely. The deep red trim of the windows had held up better. If it was supposed to make any New Englander think of home, Banks surmised, the hundred-plus degrees and zero humidity would negate the effect.

Some figures were moving around the jail, so he decided to make that his first stop on the tour of the town. A Mexican, an Indian, and Edwin Brody were working pieces of the broken wall into a water trough, then placing them on the wall as if trying to assemble a puzzle, which in fact they were. Then one would push dust and wet mud into the fissure. All three were filthy, and only the Mexican labored in a shirt.

"Scary business there, Mr. Sheriff."

Brody gave him a quick glance and continued his work. "Good morning to you, Mr. Banks. You know the iron-studded door to this place is worth more than the whole damned building. It may be worth more than any two damned buildings, I suspect. Meet Juan Diego and Chief Juan Zapata Negro." The Mexican gave a brief nod, and the Indian approached with an outstretched hand.

"Me Juan Black Shoe. Good Papago, you bet. Eight Apache, dead. Juan Black Shoe friend to white American, you bet. No American kill, Apache kill, you see. You bet."

Though it might have sounded comical, Banks was impressed by the solemnity of the Papago headman. "Yes, Chief. I am Banks. Good friend, yes."

"*Usted hable español*, Banksy?"

"No, Chief. No Spanish," he returned with a smile.

"Okay, okay. Good friends *hablamos* American. You see." He returned to his work.

Banks stood quietly watching the work before saying, "Look here, Sheriff. I've done some carpentry work. I can put a one-room together that's pretty tight and can withstand the wind and rain, if you don't mind it being a little off square. I'll be glad to help."

"Call me Edwin," the lawman replied without looking up. "Thank you for your offer, but we'll be okay. And I am the constable rather than sheriff, although there cannot be much difference between the two. There's not much cause to lock up anyone, really. Be they farmer or prospector, if anyone acts up, I escort him home and tell him to sleep there until the next morning. In seven months I've pulled my pistol once, and that was to crack a drover in the head." He stopped his work. "Well, I've done that twice now. Let me explain that first one. He was in the Sam Houston, purposely insulting some women. There's always people coming and going, and there's always three or four wives. And then some Mexicans come from Santa Ynez and bring their women with them. Anyway, that drover acted out, and we won't stand for having the ladies insulted."

"Oh, I understand. You don't owe me an explanation for your duty. But I thought all the Mexicans drank at the cantina—the other end of town y'all mentioned yesterday."

"All Fuerte Viejo Mexicans drink at La Cantina. Those from Santa Ynez...well, for the most part, they're old established families.

55

They come over here. I can't explain it, really. Maybe just a higher social class." If Juan Diego were insulted, he gave no indication.

"So all the women here are married, are they? No dance hall queens doesn't bode well for me."

Brody gave a hearty guffaw. "Ha! If that's what you're looking for, let's go see Big Sarah!"

CHAPTER 19

SATURDAY AFTERNOON

"What in hell is a Big Sarah?"

Edwin Brody finally looked up and met the newcomer's eyes. "Well...hold on." He turned to Chief Juan Zapato Negro and Juan Diego. *"Diez minutos, por favor. Hablamos con Sarah."* He reached for a white shirt that was stained so evenly that it appeared to have been manufactured brown. The other men laughed, which made Banks more than a little self-conscious. The chief rattled off something unintelligible while the mirth disappeared from his face. Whatever was about to happen, he clearly disapproved. Brody, however, laughed again, and finishing buttoning his shirt, he led his Anglo companion across the wide expanse of street.

"Mr. Sheriff, what's this all about? I can't help but think that y'all are having a laugh at my expense."

"Call me Edwin, I said. And of course we are laughing, but not at you, friend. Straight ahead is my room." In a few seconds they were there, and the lawman reached through the open doorway and pulled a clear bottle off an unseen shelf. Splashing a few drops of liquid onto his finger, he spread it around his neck, unwittingly smearing the adobe from his fingers onto his neck, hair, and cheeks. He looked worse than before. It smelled of cinnamon water. "We've got precious little to laugh at around here," he said as if the conversation had not paused. It spooked Banks somewhat and caused him even more trepidation. Despite the lawman's quiet nature, he thought conversation might help.

"Edwin, I've been in the territory for close to a year, and I do not think I will ever get used to this heat. It's like stoking the furnace of a paddle-wheeler. The ground, the buildings—everything gives off heat. It's like standing next to an oven. It is worse here than at Whipple and Prescott."

"Did you come here from California or the old Butterfield route?"

"Neither. I came through the Beale road used by the Santa Fe Stage Company. So few passengers I am certain that business has ceased on that road. But it was hot too. It is just too much to bear."

"I like it," answered Brody solemnly. "It's preparing me."

The response puzzled Banks, but before he could inquire further, he was cut off.

"Let's head up the street and turn right," Brody said firmly, all previous traces of mirth were gone. "Big Sarah is a business-woman, a working girl. Why, she's the best baker in the whole territory, I bet. She is white, but she has learned to cook pies using the fruit of the saguaros and prickly pear, just like the Papagos. Just like old Chief Juan's people back there. They're good too. The pies, I mean. You know, apples shipped from Texas or farther east cost too damned much, and sugar is hard to come by too. But she gets it done."

"Are you taking me to buy pie?"

"Maybe I'm showing you the town," answered Brody with a wide sweep of his arm. They swung right into the second and only other street in town. To Banks's left was a row of squalid one- and two-room houses. They appeared to offer some shelter, but only the barest minimum. None were square, and all had gaps or cracks in the boards. Banks took note that there was little adobe, and that the lumber, as old as dirt in appearance, could not have been more than twenty or twenty-five years old, probably shipped from

Mexico. He was not sure that the timber of the Prescott area had been accessible at the time in question. Like the Nantucket Whaler, the extreme elements of Sonora had weathered these as well.

To the right were the remnant walls of an old mission. Spread out in what must have been larger rooms at one time, the dusty brown walls ranged from eight feet to just knee high. He was surprised that despite its lack of use, there was no creosote, scrubby thorn, or other of the desert growths that sprang up from nowhere in a land quite seemingly hostile to flora and fauna. Maybe the few brown *niños* from the Mexican section used it as an area to play games. If there was a priest, though Banks was unaware of one, then maybe he kept the grounds tidy.

A few seconds more, a few more steps in the dusty, crunchy gravel, and they stood in front of a dilapidated L-shaped house. Though it had been whitewashed at one time, it had not seen a recent application, and there was as much exposed wood as painted. Banks thought it was the finest house in Fuerte Viejo, though that was like calling it the best acre of muck in an entire Louisiana swamp. No self-respecting person from anywhere east of the Mississippi would have deigned to live in any house on the street. The places were little better than what he had seen of slave cabins, but he would not say as much to Brody. No, he would be a good guest in town.

Brody approached the picket wire fence that surrounded the meager lot. "Hello the house!"

"Hello back!" came a voice from within, and a young woman, tall, big-boned yet pretty, stepped out to the porch. "Edwin Brody, you never visit me." She stood with hands on her hips and gave a wicked grin. "And when you do come, you think you have to bring reinforcements with you!"

"Sarah, please welcome mister...?"

"McLeroy Banks, ma'am," interrupted the suddenly eager companion. "From Prescott and Fort Whipple as of late. I am pleased to make your acquaintance." He gave a broad sweep of his black hat. Any previous hesitation had dissipated.

"Well, do come in, Mr. Fancy-Talking Banks. Get acquainted and let me find out more about you." As she waved him onto the porch, she never stopped smiling, and her whole countenance was one of joy. "And you, Mr. Brody?"

"Not for me, Sarah. You know me and my respect for the bonds of matrimony." He grinned.

"Matrimony!" screamed Banks. He stood motionless on the tiny porch before leaping back into the patch of dirt that was a yard.

"We're not going to get...well, who's married?"

The constable guffawed and Big Sarah did so even louder. Her ample frame was bent double at the waist. "Please, Edwin! Don't scare him so," she managed to say through her laughter.

Banks was now at his limit. He was suddenly as angry as he had been eager but a moment before. "What the hell kind of place is this? What's going on?"

Involuntarily his right hand curled into a fist, and he stepped toward his companion. Big Sarah, conscious of his movements or not, grasped his arm and pulled him to her. "No harm, sir. Come on inside and we will get acquainted. I will tell you all about Old Pete and everything will be fine. I promise you." She steered him toward the open door.

"You do that, Sarah," said Brody through a wheezing laugh. "Be sure and tell him about that libertine Old Pete." He thought about returning to the meager jail to repair that wall but decided to go to his jacal instead. As he walked, he cast his eyes along the small-framed huts so as to not see the mission ruins. Even in trying to avoid the Bad Thought, its presence cast its shadow over him.

CHAPTER 20

SATURDAY NIGHT

Banks stared at the peeling ceiling and surmised that the whitewash had been cut with water and applied long ago. He popped his lips. "Well, now, there is something in this burgh after all!"

Sarah gave a pleasant and meaningless laugh. "What treasure are you looking for, Mr. Banks?"

He turned his head to face Sarah. "At this point the treasure is in the looking for it. Most of my jobs are fifty cents a day or room and board. No real future for me in that. But I'm working on something."

"Something that is going to pave your street with gold here in old Fuerte Viejo?" she asked, seemingly ignorant of the redundancy. "You'd better chart another course, sailor."

"Well, miss, uh…?"

"I think the way we are, you can just call me Sarah." She laughed. "Hard to be formal when you are in God's own."

"Okay, Sarah. But I'm working on something now. The Walpais and Yavapais and every other kind of Pai made up north too dangerous. But what I am working on here in this burgh, it's not going to get me rich, but I will be able to work from a different angle, one that up to this point has been closed off."

She replied with a hint of sarcasm, "You left Prescott 'cause it was full of Indians? You've heard of Apaches, right? And this path to riches sounds mysterious. Most men here tell me about some phantom mine, some hidden ore deposit, or how they are waitin' for the Apaches to be shied away so that they can run a thousand head of Texas cattle on the grasslands. But you're a mystery man."

He rolled his body over to face her, and the old iron bed protested his movement. He waited for the squealing metal to stop. "Sarah, I do not think the Apaches—or Indians anywhere—will be a problem forever. Either they will be hunted to ruin or they will accept a reservation. When that happens, this land will fill up fast. It has good grass for cattle south of here and up north too. It is good weather for the constitution of the body, mining concerns, a railroad to California, and maybe river traffic down the Colorado at Yuma. I can do every job there is, and there'll be a need for workers. Santa Ynez will expand, and if I can get hold of some land, maybe I can get rid of it for a higher price.

"And you, Sarah, how and why are you here?"

"'Cause I'm with Old Pete, and this is where Old Pete wanted to wander. He works the ore, and I bake pies and do other things."

"And are you happy with that, Sarah? You sound a little sad."

"Old Pete protects me from the worst of life and I cook and clean for him, and it works for us. It is just a matter of comfort. He knows what goes on and he don't mind. Only he don't allow it when he's in town." She hesitated. "And don't call him my pimp. It's not like that." She suddenly became modest and pulled the dingy sheet to her chin. "You have not said how long you have been west, but let me tell you, things are different out here. The men are lonely, and us women are too. It's all so very hard. We work with each other, that's all. Do not judge me, Mr. Banks."

"How can I judge you or anyone? Miss Sarah, I am not one to throw stones. Do not expect me to look down on you, your arrangement, or your conduct. That is not me. I just live my life and try not to hurt others. That is why I inquire of this Old Pete. If you tell me that you're not married, then I think we are all in good standing." He looked at her solemnly. "I promise never to hurt you. Just let me know I'll have a chance to romance you, and that you will stay here for as long as I do."

She flung the sheet aside and ran her hands over her stomach, beating on it like a drum for a moment. "I'm in Fuerte Viejo, so this is where it is going to be. Now, tell me about your new path to riches and glory."

Banks laughed and reached to pull her more closely to him. The bed attempted its role as chaperone and tried to quell the mood with its protesting agony. "Maybe in a bit, but for now I want to know if the rate is for an hour or for a poke. My pocketbook wants to know."

CHAPTER 21

SUNDAY MORNING

Walking Knife was furious. When he made it back to the family group—*if* he made it back—he would stay there and send Red Buffalo Calf back to the Mescaleros alone. He felt obligated to return his friend to safe territory and that was all. And friend was a very strong word to use at this point. He stopped and scanned the terrain in all directions. There was no sign of movement, not even smoke from any lone cabin. The soldiers who chastised all the People, friend or foe of his own band, and the miners who scratched the ground for hard metal rock were all absent today. That was good. Also, it was very odd. Despite the continual conflict between the races, this part of Apacheria was filling with white people. There had been too many of them before the white man's war, and while they had vacated during that time, now they were back in even bigger numbers. Hopefully he could get to a camp of friendly Pinals, and they would give up enough corn and meat to get the two travelers home. Although he had explored this area previously, he did not know where water and game could be found, for this was even beyond the area of his kinsmen, the Chiricahuas. Any friendly band would be a sight to warm his heart. In a time of severe hunger, which was soon approaching, he could eat a bird, a snake, anything with meat on it. These were things that the People held in disdain. He would eat no insects; even he had his limits. But with that feeble Red Buffalo Calf, with that sick coward who had forgotten and forsaken his training—well, eating anything taboo in front of him would simply finish him as a warrior and a man. So he hoped for Pinals.

Red Buffalo Calf walked sullenly and hugged himself. "I want to go home now. This place is full of witches and terrible things and I want to leave it. If I ever make it home, I will never go farther west than the white sands or the Rio Bravo." Occasionally he would shiver. He was hardly acting like an Inde, an Apache.

"Just tell me what you saw," demanded Walking Knife. Last night, after traveling hard all day, they had made the Place of Two Strange Men. Although few Red Paint People traveled that far west, the place was known to them. It was a bad place with bad magic. However, none from his band knew why the cabin was known to be bad. Had it always been that way, or was it because the two white men had come and brought the evil with them? Walking Knife, of course, did not believe in such. He was simply curious—had been curious. And now, thanks to that weeping Mescalero, he would never know the mystery. Though he had been to Mexico long ago, before his pledge, and had raided haciendas there and in Pinos Altos and along the Rio Grande, and had even entered some abandoned ones, he had never seen the inside of one of the whites' adobe shelters when they were in use. What marvelous things might be inside?

They had agreed that long after nightfall, Red Buffalo Calf would sneak close to the cabin, while Walking Knife kept a lookout. Actually, Red Buffalo had done quite well. There had been a large amount of white-man tools and debris in the yard, but he had managed to work his way through quickly yet quietly to an open window. No animal had stirred during his approach. Then, carrying a knife to push aside the cloth that hung in the window, he had crept to the west window and looked in and had seen something that suddenly caused him to cease being an Apache. He let out a wail that turned into a scream and then ran back with no thought of the tools in the yard. He made such a loud clanking and banging that one Indian sounded like ten white men. But Red Buffalo Calf would not describe what he had seen. He must have truly believed it to be evil.

"Just say it," Walking Knife had repeated.

"No! My friend, I will not speak of it. I will sit in a smoke lodge for one hundred days and take nothing but water. But I will not speak of this again. To do so would be much worse than eating the flesh of Grandfather Bear." He clawed at the sides of his head as if the memory were a physical veil that he could pull away.

So was that it? he wondered. If they had been eating a bear, that would not have been so disturbing. Even one of the People might eat a bear if he was not a believer, or if he was too hungry to go farther. The great warrior Nana had eaten a bear, and he was not looked down upon or chastised. Maybe the two witches were eating a man. He tried to imagine the inside of the white men's lodge and how one might prepare a Papago, Pima, or Pinal on a spit or cook pot. Maybe, but whatever had been seen had ruined a potentially good warrior. Or maybe Red Buffalo Calf, who had only recently completed his fourth raid and become a warrior, had not received adequate training, had not been toughened to the ways of a warrior. Mescalero training was probably quite different than Mimbreno training.

Walking Knife looked over at his friend and shook his head. Next time he would bring Zuni Wife, Silver Horn, or Sleepy, or he would travel alone. His tired and lonesome companion continued to hold himself, shake his head, and mutter.

CHAPTER 22

SUNDAY EVENING

Edwin Brody, Peter Heydt, Juan Diego, and some Mexicans were in a loose mass just beyond La Cantina. Heydt sat on a wooden bench by the corral, huddled over a checkerboard and considering his next move but also keeping an eye on the thunderheads to the west. They were a curious blend of gray and purple, and ominously, they pushed a not-so-subtle wind before them. The wind minimally alleviated the furnace heat. Although he had been watching storms all of his life, he had never contemplated the amount of time between arrival and departure. He surmised, though, that the rain would bypass Fuerte Viejo and Santa Ynez and dump its much-needed moisture before it reached the Apache lands in and around Fort Bowie.

Heydt chose not to make a jump and moved a single man to the side of the board. He turned again to the west and studied the storm. Rain in the desert was a double-edged sword. It brought life to the fields around town, and it caused a profusion of flowers in the Sonoran landscape beyond. But if the rain came too fast and too strong, the hard soil of the mountain would crumble away, and the boulders of the high ground would tumble and threaten the village below. Dry arroyos could turn into death-dealing rivers without warning. Several years ago, before the Anglo presence, long before his own arrival, three young boys from the village had been playing in the first big wash to the north when a storm pushed back from the east. They knew to go home but thought they had time enough. They were wrong. The only survivor told the village of a great roar. He told them of an old dead tree, probably a mesquite, that had been the front wall of a deluge of water that had swept away the other two children. A lengthy search had turned up only one, battered and broken and very much dead, half buried and a mile away. Only buzzards had guided those looking for the boys. One was lost and one was found, and nobody knew which was which due to the damage of the body. From that point, Father Esteban had decided to ring the mission bell when storms neared, to serve as notice that everyone should return to the village. Now, as was custom, in the last gasps of afternoon, the bell pealed its warning.

Brody sat on the fence rail watching the game, or trying to. Perhaps it was the humidity that the storm was bringing that weighed so oppressively on him, but he suspected that the Bad Thought was near. As he faced north, the mission was in his line of sight, so he shielded his eyes with his right hand and tried to tuck his head into his chest to make himself smaller. He also raised his shoulders to help with the task. Was it a weight on him or just trying to avoid the mission? He groaned inwardly. The Bad Thought was certainly coming.

"No more, Señor Pete?" asked Felipe Lopez, Heydt's opponent. He was not quitting but rather keeping an eye on the weather as well.

"*No más, Felipe.*" He nodded his head westward. "*Mañana, possible.*"

Two other Mexicans moved around the corral, attempting to get the horses to the cover of the ramada. One, a big and meaty roan, was being decidedly difficult. Brody slid off his perch on the topmost fence rail to lend a hand. Before he could twist his gun belt into a more comfortable position, Bendix peered his heavy frame around the corner of the cantina. He was out of breath.

"There you are! Brody, there's trouble in the saloon. There's a man in there causing a ruckus and looking for a fight. He's already hurt Spencer."

Having whirled around, Brody stood looking at Bendix with some fear. He regretted having given the man his attention. If he'd just kept his eyes on the corral, with his back to the big bastard, no fear would have been visible. He hated giving Bendix notice anyway. There was some enjoyment in ignoring this self-important bug. However, he had lost that little battle already. He worked his fists in clenches.

"Which saloon?"

"Why, my saloon, goddammit! Why would I give a goddamn what happens in the Sam Houston? And you'd better hurry. I think it's Greybib Calhoun."

"Don't tell me—"

"Greybib Calhoun!" Heydt leapt up. "I've seen him, Brody."

The lawman quickly forgot his ire with Bendix and gave his attention to the usually unperturbed Heydt.

"Edwin," Heydt continued, "he's tough. Once, in Mesilla, I saw him beat two mean near to death. He's not scared of going to jail." Heydt suddenly realized why he was concerned about the storm being a portent of danger: he had left his Henry rifle at the Haslett Brothers Express office. "Let me go get my rifle and some of the miners and we'll go together."

"There's no time for that! I said he's already hurt Spencer!" screamed Bendix. He was turning red and breathing even faster.

Brody shook his head at Pete Heydt and turned to face up the street toward the Nantucket Whaler. "Thanks, but no. No sense in other people getting hurt doing what I'm paid to do." He turned to head north to the Nantucket Whaler, but he did not advance. He took a deep breath and gave a long hard stare at the saloon. But he did not move.

CHAPTER 23

LATER SUNDAY EVENING

Despite Brody's admonition, Heydt took off for the Haslett Brother's Express building at a run. Micah, ever pushing his broom, straightened his spectacles and hailed him.

"What's the hurry there, Peter, boy? Some of the fellas come back to town, you know?"

Heydt barely slowed to answer. "Stay put, Micah. Stay put in there and don't come out."

From down the street, Brody watched him run, but he knew that it was not cowardice. Good, calm Peter Heydt. He was going to get his Henry rifle regardless of the circumstance, and regardless of his instructions not to get involved.

The constable hitched up his gun belt and slipped the leather thong from the hammer. He met the eyes of the others, but they said nothing. After several seconds Bendix broke the silence.

"Well...what's it gonna be, Edwin?"

In response Brody placed his palm on the grip of the big Remington and stared hard at Bendix, who raised both hands in protest. "Not here, man! The fight's not here with me!"

Brody said nothing but began his march to the Nantucket Whaler. When he heard footsteps and heavy breathing behind him, he turned to see the saloon keeper in tow. "No sense in your coming. If you were too scared to handle it yourself, you're too scared to be a part of it now. Stay back and out of my way." Bendix turned and headed back around La Cantina.

Now, as he began again, there was no noise but the crunch of his boots on the hard gravel. He looked down as he worked his way up the street, mesmerized by the cadence. And like in La Cantina the night he hit the Hombre, time and space were distorted. Another loud noise came in conjunction with his foot hitting the wooden boardwalk of the jail. He stopped and gazed across the street to see Old Micah, broom in hand, struggling to keep it in his grip and operate his heavy door. Micah gave one very nervous glance over his shoulder before stepping inside and sliding the bolt.

Old fool. Locking the door sure won't keep the bullets from entering. More somberly he reflected, *What if that's my last thought? What if the ridicule of Micah is it before the blackness comes?* Then he caught sight of the chapel and continued his short trek. *God, if you are there, this sinner needs you.*

Then before he knew it and before he was ready, he was at the entrance to the saloon. This was too quick! He had not prepared himself; there had been no time to think. *I'll go in on the three. One...two...three. No, no, this time. One...two...three!* He drew a deep breath, took the heavy piece of iron from his holster, and pushed through the swinging door.

From down the street, Beverly Harvill watched him enter and hurried inside her shop and knelt before her stuffed chair. She began to pray silently but fervently.

CHAPTER 24
LATER SUNDAY EVENING

There was too much for Brody to absorb when he stepped inside the Nantucket Whaler. A prone figure lay on the floor, and just beyond, in front of the bar, a larger man held Billy the barkeep by the collar at arm's length. Billy was small, but still the man showed great strength as the helpless victim's feet were off the floor. The big man turned to face the new arrival, dropping Billy in the process and revealing two pistols of different size in his belt. To the left, opposite the bar, a man in a loud red shirt arose from his table, a shiny brass Henry repeating rifle held across his body. Without speaking, Brody raised the Remington at arm's length, and an enormous boom filled the room. A geyser of blood erupted across the table as Red Shirt took two steps back and collapsed face up on the hard floor. A third man sitting at the same table, dressed in a pale blue paisley, stared down in awe at his dead companion and then leapt to his feet, arms reaching unnaturally high as if he was quite literally reaching for the sky. Everyone's ears were still ringing from the pistol shot as the scared man spoke. "Don't shoot, sir! Don't do it!"

From another table McLeroy Banks calmly walked over, reached down for the Henry, and held it at his waist. Brody then turned his attention back to the bar and Greybib Calhoun. He took a step forward, pistol still in front of him, and took a quick peek at the prone figure. It was Spencer. Next to him was a beer mug split lengthwise from top to bottom.

"You do this?"

"Yeah," Greybib said with a deep drawl. It came out in two syllables to indicate a subtle chuckle. His hands were half-heartedly in the air. "Broke it right over his head." The smirk was pure arrogance. Despite just seeing a companion killed, the cowman was supremely confident.

The lawman switched the pistol to his left hand and picked up the mug piece with his right. With a sudden and unexpected explosion, Brody took two steps and threw his right hand so hard and with such fury and momentum that he left his feet. There was no smack of fist hitting tissue. The glass mug made no sound at all, but Calhoun wailed before spinning and collapsing to his knees. The big man wanted to scream, but he could only gnash his teeth. He wanted to grab his face, but he was afraid of what he might touch. It felt like fire. Before he could collect himself, the butt of the Remington cracked into his forehead at the hairline. More pain.

"Stand up, you son of a bitch. You stand up right goddamned now."

Again, Greybib attempted to collect himself. He went from knees to one foot and then finally the other foot. Wobbling and without conscious thought, he raised his hands in surrender. Clearly the fire and arrogance were dissipating, if not gone. Brody took the pistol and pressed the barrel to Calhoun's pants below the belt buckle.

"Don't do that. Please don't." Greybib's face was covered in red, and a strip of cheek flopped as he spoke.

"Billy! You got a whoopin' stick behind the bar. Take just the hardest swing you got and knock this son of a bitch in the head."

Billy hesitated.

"Do it, Billy. Do what I say."

"Mr. Bendix don't allow me to touch the stick," he said quietly. He was thoroughly terrified and overwhelmed by it all.

"Damn it, Billy! You bust his head or I'll blast his pecker off. I'll blast his pecker right into the woodwork." Brody's lips were back and he snarled the words like an actor overplaying the part, hamming up the role of an angry man. But it was not an act. His heels were rising and lowering in alternating movement.

"Please, mister." Calhoun's eyes were closed. "Please don't shoot. Please don't do that." The words came out in a whisper. Blood had covered his face now and was soaking the nasty collar of his namesake. Not knowing what else to do, Billy ran for the door and kept going. In response Brody pulled the hammer back, and there was a prominent click. The man in the blue shirt, arms still high, turned to Banks with pleading eyes. Banks calmly and with no emotion shook his head. Blue Shirt tried to speak but his voice broke. "Sir, please. We will leave and never come back, sir."

The click of the pistol cocking and the words from his friend caused Greybib to open his eyes. Though he had felt the barrel's pressure in his groin, he now saw it too. Blood continued to pour from his forehead and cheek and was now covering the chest and shoulders of the shirt. Its once gray appearance now looked navy blue with the blood it had soaked. But it could absorb no more and was now collecting red on the surface. It spattered on the floor when he bent forward to see his predicament. With his renewed realization came terror.

"Oh God, no! Please don't shoot! Please!" He blinked furiously in a vain attempt to clear his eyes of the sticky blood. They appeared so very white on his crimson face. The words came out in sobbing gasps. "Good God, please don't shoot my pecker off. Pleeeease." His dark gray pants grew even darker at the crotch as his bladder released. He was sobbing and his face was twisted in anguish. His whole head was a red mess, and along with the strip of hanging flesh, a long strand of mucous hung from his nose.

Brody's ears were filling with the familiar roar that accompanied rage, but he was aware of soft footsteps approaching. "Edwin." Peter Heydt placed a firm hand on his shoulder. "It's over, Edwin. It's done."

While Greybib Calhoun wailed and sobbed and shook, Brody lowered the barrel to just below the cloth. Then he fired.

CHAPTER 25

SUNDAY DUSK

Banks had taken two pistols from the semiconscious Calhoun and was still carrying the Henry rifle when he escorted the dazed gunman and Blue Shirt from the front door of the Nantucket Whaler. Blue Shirt's eyes were wide and vacant, and Calhoun had said nothing since the pistol ball grazed his crotch, leaving a stain of black powder in the urine-soaked denim. Their arms, though both down, were in contrast, as the latter's hung limply and the former seemed as if he did not know how to carry his—crossing them, putting hands on hips, then letting them dangle. He fumbled for something to occupy his hands, but of course there was nothing. As the small trio stepped under the veranda by the hitching post, Banks broke the uncomfortable silence.

"What's your name?"

"Me, sir?" answered Blue Shirt. "Carter. Phin Carter."

"And where are you from, please, Carter?"

"Virginia, sir. Well, I'm from Virginia, but I lived in Kentucky and Ohio too. All over, maybe."

When there were no further questions, Carter turned as ashen as his companion was deep crimson. Had the questions been a macabre, cruel twist to relax him before execution? He turned to look for condolence, but Calhoun had absorbed nothing and remained mute.

"Are you gonna kill us now?"

It was Banks now who was truly stunned. His mouth hung open as if he had just been slapped. "Am I going to kill you? Well, now, that is the damnedest thing I have heard today—and a very strange day at that. Damnedest thing I have heard. It is my intent to get you out of this town as you are now. There's no further bloodshed if I can help it. We're here now to put you on your horses."

"Thank you mightily!" The weight of the world flew from Carter's shoulders. "This is..." He hesitated. "I don't know what this is. Thanks for your kindness, sir." He stepped down to put Greybib on his big bay, doing most of the effort himself. The big man was now next to useless. Another bolus of mucous was hanging from his nose and lips. He was oblivious.

"You know what you've got there." Carter indicated the two revolvers stuck in the band of Banks's waist. "Those are Thunder and Lightning."

"How is that again?"

"Thunder and Lightning. Thunder's the big one, and the little Wells Fargo pistol is Lightning. Most people in Santa Ynez know of 'em. Greybib's had those two since I met him on the Brazos. From there to Mesilla to Santa Ynez."

Banks shrugged. "They do not mean much to me. None of my concern—unless you're quaintly telling me that he is going to try and come back later and fetch them. That what you are doing?"

"No, sir. I am saying that policeman is the bravest and toughest man I have ever seen. He's tougher than any keelboat man. Those two pistols are trophies. And anybody who gets that policeman's Remington is someone I do not hope to ever meet. God's truth." He paused to grab the saddle horn and pull himself up onto his horse. "Are we to travel back to Santa Ynez unprotected? What if we are molested by brigands or Apaches?"

Banks rested a weary frame on the pillar of the veranda. Though he was unaware of the science, the adrenaline that had raced through him moments ago was now leaving him and he felt terribly weak. "Mr. Carter. You will have to travel without weapons, as you have abused the privilege of having them. You are brigands yourselves and have come here with black hearts. Indians, as I know them and have heard, do not fight at night. So you may ride to Santa Ynez or to hell, I care not which. But let me say this: I am new to Fuerte Viejo and not acquainted with its inhabitants. But the town constable, this policeman, scares me. He is a forthright but dangerous man. If you two come here again, I do not doubt but that he will kill you both. Do not come back ever."

Carter, mounted on his own pinto, led Calhoun's horse away from the hitching post and a few feet into the street. Then he swatted the bay's rump with his hat and looked up to see it bolt for north of town and beyond. He turned to look solely upon Banks.

"Sir," he said with his first smile, a relaxed one. "I promise you that I cannot answer for him. You know that I can't. But know that I am now headed to Mesilla or California and that I will not pass this way again." He dug in his spurs and with another swat proceeded after the late Tiger of Santa Ynez.

CHAPTER 26

SUNDAY NIGHT

The sun was down fully now, and Banks exited the Nantucket Whaler yet again with his right arm held before him to ward off contact with anyone on the street. In his left, but also held away from his body, was the Henry rifle that just a short time before had been held by Greybib Calhoun's dead companion. He looked up and down the street, but no crowd had emerged to question the shooting. There were Mexicans moving around on the south side of town, and here and there the dull glow of a lamp bled out from some of the Anglo dwellings. At Brody's adobe jacal, a faint golden beam emerged from a window and cast a minor pale intrusion into the growing darkness. He strode there purposefully but cautiously, as if the rifle were a bomb.

Inside the small, cell-like room he was surprised to see a beautiful and petite blond woman and a stout Mexican señora. Nobody spoke when he entered, but they did acknowledge his presence with a nod before returning their attentions to Edwin Brody, who lay on the bed with his body curled into a tight ball, his back to the other occupants. To Banks it seemed as if the room was suffocating it was so hot.

"Edwin, there's something you need to see."

"I do not wish to see anything. Please go away," he whispered. He attempted to curl himself even more tightly.

"No, sir, you are going to see this. Look at me."

The blonde began to interject, while the big Mexican stared at him with eyes wide. "Mister," began the pretty one.

"Banks. McLeroy Banks."

"Well, Mr. Banks, I will not tolerate rudeness here. Our dear constable has—"

"Killed a man!" interrupted Banks. It came out abruptly and rudely.

Hearing it out loud and in such a manner caused Brody to groan and stir from his malaise. With a fingertip he scratched at a small hole in the adobe, then turned to look up with eyes glassy and red from strain. Banks shoved the rifle in his face, and the policeman turned his gaze to take in the piece. His eyes moved up and down the weapon several times before they locked on the hammer.

"Do you see that, sir?" asked Banks. "The hammer is back." Brody nodded with eyes still wide and his mouth solemn and flat.

"Edwin, this gun was cocked and ready to fire. Those men were here to kill you. When you entered that saloon, you were dead where you stood. I thought you needed to know that. You were good enough to save your own life. Maybe that doesn't help with how you feel, but in my eyes you did good. Really good."

The lawman reached for the rifle and held it briefly and with trepidation, as if it was an item of filth, then gave it back. "I knew that, I did. And yet I did not know it." His breath was just a whisper. Clearly he was strained terribly by the night's events. "I acted without thinking. The whole thing just happened and I don't know how. It was fear and hatred, and now one man is dead and one man is hurt." His head snapped up with sudden realization. "Anyone else? Did I hurt anyone else?" Suddenly he stood. "Oh my God! I forgot about Spencer. Is he okay?"

"No, sir, nobody else is hurt. That Spencer must have a headache, but he left out on his own and with his own legs. I don't know where he went, but I guess somebody here, somebody that knows where he might be, needs to make an account of his constitution. But know this—you saved a life tonight. You saved your own life, and who is to say that maybe you didn't save someone else's? That big man had Spencer in a bad way, and the barkeep boy too. You also saved the life of that big nasty man. You sure did. Many other lawmen might have killed him, and with good reason. But you got him under control and he lives now. They came here looking for trouble and they found it—damned sure found it." Banks leaned in unnaturally close to emphasize his point. "They wanted trouble. You hear me? They wanted trouble, and what they got was of their own making. This is not your fault. Ain't your fault in anyone's eyes."

The blonde stepped forward. "But why, Mr. Banks? Why would they come here?"

"Ma'am, I cannot answer that. I surely cannot. Could be they were bad men, and it could be they were looking for trouble. That cocked rifle tells me something."

Brody wiped his face with both hands, and again Banks was conscious of the overwhelming heat in the jacal. It was stifling. The two lamps were pouring out heat that found no exit in the tiny room. The lawman spoke. "Please excuse me. McLeroy Banks, this is Beverly Harvill. She is our tailor, seamstress, and the conscience of our town. And this is Mariana, who is my right hand and to whom I owe everything."

"It is a pleasure to meet you, Mr. Banks. I hope you will please call me Verly."

Mariana smiled broadly. "It is with much pleasure. Miss Verly, she wants to know why. Me too."

"We may never know." He turned to Edwin Brody again. "I just wanted to make sure that you are okay, Edwin. I want to see that you are absolved of guilt—not from the law, but from yourself."

"Thank you, friend. Like I said, I knew what was going on, even without really knowing. But one thing helps me. No, make that three things: I have three friends who care for my welfare."

81

CHAPTER 27

MONDAY NOON

Lieutenant Barzaga wiped his profusely sweating brow with the sleeve of his tunic. The dark fabric was crusty with salt and sand, but its abrasiveness was countered by the patina of moisture on his skin. The sun beat down out of a clear blue sky, and as it met the glaring white and pale red landscape on all sides, he thought that it was as beautiful as any painting. He stood in the stirrups and studied his troops strung out ahead and behind. This was just what he had preached and railed against, for a marauding band of Apaches, on horse or afoot, could easily wipe out the command that was scattered over the one hundred yards of desert. They were an impossible lot. No pride enthused them and no fear of discipline intimidated them. Much farther ahead he could see Corporal Batista racing back on his beautiful black steed. It was a magnificent animal, and Batista was a talented rider. They rode through the scrub brush as if it was a trail they had ridden countless times. They were fluid.

Batista pulled his horse up short, throwing up a cloud of white alkali. He saluted crisply. "Lieutenant, sir, an American waits at the border. The wagon is with him."

Barzaga threw back a salute in an offhand manner but with eyes wide in surprise; clearly this news was shocking. The wagon was to be at Tumulca. Why had the American taken it below the border? The corporal waited patiently, or tried to wait without showing his impatience, while the lieutenant unscrewed the canteen and took a slow swig. He knew his officer was digesting the news, which, granted, was as important as it was unexpected. However, it was all he could do to disguise his impatience. His black horse felt the emotion through its rider and shuffled its feet in eagerness.

"This concerns me, Corporal."

But Batista did not reply. Despite being bereft of education, he knew rhetorical statements and questions, even if he did not know that they were called such.

"Yes, this gives me great concern, Corporal," the officer repeated, and again wiped his brow. "How many miles to the wagon?"

"Perhaps five miles, sir. Maybe as much as seven. It is hard to tell in this area."

"I cannot imagine why this gringo would be so accommodating as to bring his wagon farther south. Are you sure it was him, Corporal?"

"I am certain, sir. As I rode near, he waved a flag to get my attention. I think that is foolish to do, but what other wagon would be here like that in the desert? I will approach him if you wish, sir."

"Yes, you are right. I do not like it, but you are correct. Go back and tell him that the troops will arrive in twenty minutes." He gave another look ahead and behind and then gave an exasperated sigh. "No, tell him we will arrive in forty minutes."

CHAPTER 28
MONDAY AFTERNOON

B endix sat down at the dilapidated old table at the trading post in Tumulca and poured a glass of amber rum. He deserved it, he thought, after the duty that bastard O'Meara had given him. Bringing a wagon alone through hostile Apache country was a fool's errand. A lone rider was easy prey, and a loaded wagon was easy goods. "Well, I'll be a rich fool in time enough," he said. *And a living fool,* he thought. After yesterday, he wanted to get out of Fuerte Viejo in a hurry and stay out. As soon as he heard the second shot and saw Brody leave out the front door of the saloon, he knew what had happened: the whole plan had gone south. He had run like a spreading fire to get to the wagon and get it hitched and on the road. Maybe that new man, Banks, had interfered. He had been in the saloon at that time. When he got back, if he got back, he would stay in his hotel and not venture out for anything. Anyway, he had today to think of.

That greaser lieutenant had kicked up quite a fuss about the location of the wagon but he had left pretty well satisfied. Hell, he should have been, it was less work for them. Since when did fat greasers complain about less work? But whatever happened now, it would be on the Mexican side of the border. Yep, any trouble now would be off of territorial soil. That was good. Grudgingly, he agreed that O'Meara was smart like that, at least in this case. Reluctantly, he had to salute O'Meara's brilliance. Whatever the Yankee bastard touched was golden, like that King Midas. However, the touch had not affected Brody yet. Okay, Greybib Calhoun had been a bust too. But otherwise O'Meara was smart and always planning. And again, he thought, when the crumbs fell from Farrell's plate, he would be there to snatch them. It was easy money as long as he did not have to drive another wagon deep into the Sonoran desert. And it was easy money as long as he did not have to set Brody up. Upon reflecting on that idea, he topped off his glass. Maybe after another drink, the shaking would cease.

CHAPTER 29

MONDAY AFTERNOON

Despite all the noises the troop made, the most overwhelming feature of the trek, truly, was the silence. Yes, there was the occasional creak of saddle leather, the tap of a shod horse on stone, and the constant grind of iron wheels slipping and working their course. And although the load was securely fastened and did not slide in the wagon bed, it did bump and thud as the trail led over large rocks and gullies. Above all that, though, was the silence, the total absence of conversation. It was eerie, and they all noticed it.

Lieutenant Barzaga was, for once and at last, proud of his troopers. That the American wagon driver, Bindiz, would make delivery miles farther south than had been agreed upon concerned him greatly. And it apparently worried the men too. The troopers, used to his insults and encouragement, had finally and voluntarily heeded his calls for discipline. They sensed, or at least he thought they sensed, that something was out of the ordinary. At the entrance to the shallow canyon, he had ordered them to prime their heavy infantry rifles (only better units around Mexico City received cavalry carbines) and to be prepared for anything. The order was given calmly, and the men had responded without hesitation. They rode in a column of twos, with Dominguez driving the wagon and Corporal Batista, ever-competent Batista, riding through the narrow canyon to scout ahead.

Farther up he could see Batista trotting toward him. Uncustomarily, the corporal threw off a salute and said quickly, "Lieutenant, sir, up ahead, at about one kilometer, you can see that the canyon wall has collapsed. There, to the left. There are many footprints, but I cannot determine how long they have been there. I think they are very fresh. But I rode up and scouted around the left side, up on top of the canyon. It is maybe fifteen feet high. There have been men there, but I do not see them now."

"Is it safe, Corporal?"

"I cannot say, sir. I see signs but I do not see men. The footprints went in all directions. If there is an ambush, a horse and rider can climb that fallen embankment. But the wagon would not go there."

Barzaga raised his hand to halt the column. Standing in the stirrups, he could see that several hundred meters ahead, just as the canyon turned to the right, the opposite side had indeed collapsed. He trusted Batista. If he had not seen the men, then there were no men to be seen. Perhaps they had brushed other tracks away with creosote limbs, but Barzaga doubted that of a large group, all would be adept enough to defeat the corporal's close scrutiny. Nonetheless, he turned his horse and spoke to his command.

"Soldiers of Mexico, ready yourselves. Your rifles are ready, but make your minds ready as well. Those on the right are to observe the left side of the canyon. Those on the left are to observe the right canyon wall. If there is trouble, it will come from above, not from ahead. Forward!"

The men, reins in their left hands and rifles in their right, moved forward. All eyes were on top of the canyon walls.

CHAPTER 30

MONDAY AFTERNOON

Batista, ever cautious and knowledgeable, rode as close to the canyon wall as the terrain or outcroppings would allow. His heavy Enfield, made for Confederate infantry during the war, rested across his thighs, fully loaded and a cap in place. It was much safer, he knew, to hold the rifle upright with the butt plate on his thigh. However, if danger came, he wanted the piece horizontal and ready to bring to his cheek. Suddenly, faster than he could register, a very fat man emerged from behind the broken shelf of rock and sand and pointed a shotgun at Lieutenant Barzaga.

As they came upon the collapsed canyon wall, the lieutenant ceased scanning the right edge and peered instead to his left and at what nature had done to damage its own creation. There was a great ramp by which to escape the confinement, but it was big enough only for horse and rider. No wagon could climb—But his thought was interrupted by a short fat man emerging from behind a larger piece of rubble. It was so surprising he could barely absorb it. Then, as he realized what was happening, an eruption of flame threw him from his saddle. As he hit the ground, the air flew from him, and despite his best effort, he could not gain it back. He could not even gasp, though he knew he was trying, or at least willing himself to try. With sudden horror, a sound like the ocean filled his ears, and he knew he was going to die. The roar grew louder, overpowering some distant pops, and blackness began to envelop his vision, closing it from the outer limits until he could only see a pinprick of light surrounded by dark. Then there was nothing, not even a thought.

At the emergence of the fat man with the shotgun, the corporal raised his rifle to fire, but more figures on the opposite rim distracted him. Yet again he again raised the rifle to his cheek and picked a target, but a shadow enveloped him from behind. He turned to address it, but a hornet-like sting struck his back. He pitched from the saddle and landed awkwardly on his stomach, facing the wagon. Try as he might, he could not move himself. No muscle would respond, but curiously, the pain did not leave him. And like the sting of a giant bee, it never ceased but increased in intensity, like a burn from a cigarette. Batista's eyes moved back and forth frantically. Though the confined space was filled with rifle smoke, dust, and panicked horses, he could still discern what was happening. Los Hombres, men in big sombreros, were pouring fire from long rifles and pistols down onto the soldiers. Dominguez was crawling on all fours with blood streaming from his mouth. Concepcion was motionless on the ground, as were others whom he could not recognize. As there were fewer soldiers, the pops and booms became less frequent. But the hornet sting still burned.

One Hombre, tall and rangy, calmed the wagon horses, then turned his attention to the wagon itself. Batista saw the man's chest explode as a bullet passed through his back and through his front. A wet mist flew through the air like the spray from a waterfall, only this was dark red. That shooting was curious, as he'd thought all the soldiers were dead. That thought was interrupted by the approach of two men he could only identify as four boots adorned with enormous spurs. His state of paralysis did not allow him to look up into their faces.

"So, one of the bastards still breathes. Not for long, though."

"Hey, friend, you see what happens when Los Hombres come to visit? Maybe you bring us a gift, eh?"

The two men laughed. Then Batista felt a hot barrel against his temple. He knew what was coming, but his body would not allow him to fight it. He was helpless. He never heard the boom, just everything was gone. He ceased to be.

Gordito slung the shotgun over his shoulder and struggled to get his heavy frame up the embankment. "Hey, El Gato, we killed them all. It was not so hard. But we lost poor Nuñez—somebody popped him good. Every victory has a price, no?"

"Poor Nuñez. But he will find no more trouble in no more shit-hole jails." El Gato blew the smoke from his rifle. He had remained hidden until all was clear.

The two men shuffled down the slope and swatted the still smoky air. El Gato climbed the wagon box, then high-stepped over the buckboard seat to reach the pinewood boxes in the bed. Pulling a large Remington Army pistol, he fired two shots into the padlock. They were so loud and there was so much reverberation in the confined draw that none of the men heard the iron piece hit the wagon bed. He dragged the chain and flipped the green lid off and onto the dusty canyon floor.

"Look, my friends." He reached in and pulled out a new 1867 Winchester carbine. The shiny brass caught the sunlight and shone like gold. It reflected white glaring patterns on the faces of the men and the undersides of sombreros. "See what El Gato has provided for you." Some two dozen men smiled.

CHAPTER 31
MONDAY EVENING

It was close to dusk, and the horse bladder of water was nearing empty. There had been no running streams, only stream beds, and Walking Knife reasoned that he would have to make camp earlier than normal because of the ineffectualness of Red Buffalo Calf. He would have to select a spot, collect firewood, and again search for badly needed water. In frustration he let his mind wander back to his home with the Red Paint People. If all went well, if Red Buffalo Calf would contribute, and if they did not confront any enemies, they might be home in five days. It was a hope, anyway. But the problem, aside from Red Buffalo Calf himself, was avoiding those hostile bands or white soldiers.

Walking Knife knew that despite the earlier war far to the east, all white people were connected. There were bad men among them, but it seemed that they all liked each other as a whole. That and their ability to create things and their seemingly endless numbers made them formidable. But not all of the People were connected as such. The Red Paint People got on well with Agua Calientes and Mescaleros. The Pinals and Arivaipas were almost always friendly and rarely contentious, but sometimes an intermarriage or a family squabble caused tension and, albeit rarely, a blood feud. He had been a good guest two years ago. They had been good hosts as well. And he doubted that the corn planters far north of the Gila and Salt Rivers liked anyone. The faraway Yavapais and Hualapais were friendly to the People in their area but obviously had no kinship ties to people from the east like himself. And the Red Paint People were closely related to the Chiricahua, but he did not care for those people in Mexico. Again, he thought, they were too intertwined with those filthy Mexicans, the hair hunters and givers of poison pinole. The Janeros, under Juh and others, would trade with one village while attacking another; then they would reverse it. The Mexicans would do the same, trading or killing Apaches depending on which side of the Sierra Madres or Blue Mountains they were on. Perhaps it was all the Mexican blood in them, for with each raid by one side or another, children were captured and raised in the manner of the captors. All was treachery there.

Some families there were his kin, so when they came to visit, he was a good host. But he would never go to their land again. He had gone frequently years ago, seen it, and not enjoyed it. The ground seemed dirty. He thought that wherever he put his foot was where a lie had been told, or where one of the People, one of the Inde, had been killed. While some had lost a family member from fighting whites, all had lost family to the Mexicans. Sometimes this even occurred during a truce. So he looked forward to the Black Mountains and the Gila River country that was his home.

But he grimaced when he thought that of the sadness there as well. He was still in love with Antelope Under the Moon. She did not love him, though for a while he had thought that she did. Together they had laughed at Zuni Wife's feeble attempts to court her. This was before Zuni Wife had taken the captive Zuni woman in a raid and married her. Back then he had been known as Always in the Shade. Now she was married to Gives His Horse Water First, a Chiricahua. That warrior was pleasant, never angry, and had never been on a raid that was not successful. But Walking Knife hated him. He tried to hate Antelope Under the Moon too. Did they laugh at him now as he had laughed at Zuni Wife?

The soft whinny of a horse stirred him from his thoughts. Someone was close by in the junipers and ironwood. He knew that he had been seen but squatted on his haunches out of instinct. Red Buffalo Calf did likewise. Several figures emerged from the trees and surrounded the duo. They were obviously Inde, as indicated by their hair, dress, and distinctive soft boots. As he stood, he switched the lance to his left hand and raised his right to show that it was empty. The men lowered their bows (they were not really raised to shoot) and let their war clubs droop. Only a small number had rifles. One very tall and well-formed warrior rode out from the trees. He was the only one mounted.

"You are among the Arivaipa, the Black Rock People. We have seen you for a while. Are you from a raid? Why are you among us?"

"Greetings to you. I am from the Red Paint People, a Membreno. I am from near the white man's village of Pinos Altos. My friend is from the People of the Mountains, the Mescaleros. He is from where the flat lands begin and where there is good grass all the time and where buffalos live. He is called Red Buffalo Calf." He hesitated now. He had to explain Red Buffalo Calf's sullen and very un-Apache-like state. He did not believe in witch sicknesses, but if Red Buffalo Calf believed in it, then it was not a lie. He hoped that the culture of the Black Rock Arivaipa was accepting of such things. He also hoped that there would be no punishment for bringing sickness with them.

"My friend has a witch sickness. He thinks so. We were north of the town of Santinez and he saw something very worrisome. I am taking him home to heal. His people have a dance that is different. It is not known to my people. Our beliefs are very close, but they are not the same. Now we go home and hope we do not disturb you. We hope that this brings no danger to my cousins, the Black Rock People."

"This is a bad thing. Tell us what happened."

Just then another warrior approached the mounted headman. "Serious Face, my family knows this man. Two summers ago he was in our camp. He came and ate and drank and behaved himself. He was not rude. These things I heard but did not see. I was away killing Mexicans in Sonora. I hear he is good, so I think he must be. Because I know these things, I also know that he is called Big Eyes and Walking Knife. This Red Buffalo Calf is a stranger. He is not a man that I know. I have two brothers that married Red Paint women, but they are dead now."

Another man, short and scrawny, hailed Red Buffalo Calf. "You there. My brother, Always Frowning, married a woman of your band. A sickness came and she died, but he stayed there. Always Frowning makes his home at the...Tsahmil." He attempted the word in English. "It is a white place that makes a tree into small pieces so that white people make houses. He is alone, but he likes it there. That is such a very far place. I do not go too far past the Rio Bravo."

"Ugly," interjected the mounted warrior, Serious Face. "Stop talking. If there is a man with witch sickness, we need to stay away. This is not the time to talk of other things. We must know what has happened."

Walking Knife began again. "Serious Face, we mean you no harm. This is a thing I swear. But Red Buffalo Calf will not speak. He will not tell me what he saw. He does not do this to be contrary. He is just too—"

"Enough!" Red Buffalo Calf said forcefully. "I am sorry to cause these cousins discomfort." He kept his eyes on the ground. "This is no easy thing to tell. I am embarrassed to say these things. I am young and have not seen as much as my older cousins, who are wise and brave. Please listen. I will speak of this once and that will be all."

Serious Face directed the others to prepare camp. Then he dismounted, and with Ugly and Walking Knife, he sat on the ground. Then they all listened to the story of the Place of the Two Strange Men.

CHAPTER 32

MONDAY NIGHT

Serious Face, the headman, took some dried corn from his pouch and put one or two kernels in his mouth. "This is no witch matter. It is a peculiar ritual, but I have heard of it among the People. Why a warrior does this I do not know. Maybe this brings him power. Maybe it makes him able to see at night or decide where to make camp. I have not done this, but I have heard of it. I do not think it is bad, but it is not good either. It is just simply an act. There have been men and women who have followed two paths as you describe. Perhaps no Mescalero follows this practice. Maybe you are just very young and are not aware of such things.

"We have been to the Place of Two Strange Men. That is what you call it. We call that place Where White People Are Friendly and Not Friendly. We go there frequently, as they have good water there all the time. The first time I went, we were among the rocks watching the two men. The man with hair on his face saw us. He held up his right hand to say, 'I have no weapon.' But he did this with a good rifle in his left hand. Then he held up one finger to us. As he did this, the man with no hair on his face ran inside the lodge. We did not see that one again. The one with hair on his face, who was bigger, went inside too. He is the headman. Just before he went inside, he held up his finger again. He came back out with a small bag of flour, some colored glass, and a small knife.

"We thought this was nice." He hesitated. "No, we thought it was suspicious. It was a trap, maybe. They stayed in the house and did not come out. This, we thought, meant that if we got the objects, they would shoot us. But Ugly and Watches the Horses were very brave and went and got these gifts. That is when we decided that the two men were nice. They always gave us water. No, it is better to say that they let us have water. They always left a gift for us, and we always brought a gift to them. When we raid the Pimas or the Papagos or Mexicans, we bring them corn, or a mule, or a horse. These are the things we did, and these are the things they did. But we never talked to the men, and they did not talk to us. The man with hair on his face is the one who has the camp. The one with no hair stays inside. We do not know either one."

Serious Face paused before continuing. "But for several months, things have been different. We never spoke to them and they never spoke to us, but now they do not even show themselves. They do not come out of their lodge when they see us, and they no longer give us presents. We do not know if they will allow us to have water. If we take the water, will we be shot? Why should we be afraid to get water that has always belonged to the People? They have become rude and greedy, like all white people. Maybe this ritual that you saw makes them rude. Maybe that ritual makes them invisible to us so that they are there but we do not see them. That sounds like too much magic and I cannot believe it."

Red Buffalo calf spoke next. "Thank you, Serious Face. I am glad that I did not bring harm to the Black Rock People. My people are not familiar with the ways of the whites who live here. We talk much with white people in our own home. I am glad to know that no harm will come to me, and that I have brought no harm to you."

What Serious Face said next unnerved the two travelers and filled them with apprehension. "We were going to raid the Papagos and take their cactus fruits. Now we will see the Two Strange Men. We will ask them about their magic. We will see why the two men have relations with each other."

CHAPTER 33

TUESDAY MORNING

The miner led one mule by a frayed hemp rope, and the second mule followed by a sense of obligation or perhaps just loneliness. The trio was noisier than it should have been in Apacheria. The prospector hummed, the mules brayed in annoyance, and they all kicked rocks in the loose gray gravel. It was all with a purpose, though. He reasoned that he had been seen, and he hoped that his brazen behavior would be honored by the Apaches. Perhaps they would not take sport in killing someone so brave. Maybe there was more honor in killing prey that took greater pains to hide itself. It was his only hope. It was all that he had.

The McCord homestead was just ahead. The smoke from the chimney was a thin white wisp in an otherwise clear blue sky. He wanted to appear carefree and nonchalant as he approached the home, but in truth he was in an absolute panic. He hurried while moving as slowly as he thought prudent. All the while he hoped that, should the Apaches attack, he could grab the two old Hawken muzzle-loaders and make a dash for cover. He could find a thick clump of brush and the mules would have to fend for themselves. More than likely they would end up as a stew in some wickiup. He could always come back for the ore samples. Rocks were of no value to an Indian, no matter what the tribe. Mules, though, were a delicacy.

Searching the terrain surreptitiously with his head down, he reasoned that any attack would come from his left, the higher ground. But what if the damned savages came from his right? That would be pretty cagey of them, and therefore typical, really. There had been previous encounters with them before—well, no, those had been Mohave-Apaches along the Hassayampa River, but they were all the same, sneaky and unpredictable. The only two truths were that they tortured captives unspeakably and that they would not fight after the sun went down, although he had heard that the taboo had been broken on occasion.

His trip out west with Big Sarah, through Nebraska and Wyoming to Oregon, had been fraught with danger. That was what everyone said of their trip: always "fraught" or "rife" with danger. But those Indians were of a different sort. They were Sioux, Cheyenne, Arapahos, and then finally Bannocks. They all looked alike, and all had been highly visible, with great showy displays of feathers, paint, and horsemanship. Nothing had ever happened, in retrospect, but they had seen Indians constantly, traveling on the horizon seemingly nine days out of ten. And on what must have been every fourth day, they had come into the whites' camp begging for or demanding sugar, coffee, and ammunition. Each time this had happened, the dirty savage bastards had pretended to be a new group that had not molested the immigrants previously. Filthy liars they were. But these Apaches were worse. When you saw them, it was too late. There was no waving of lances or coup sticks or any attempt to strike terror by showing bravery. No, that was for the Sioux, Cheyenne, and others. These red sons of bitches were silent, dressing like bushwhackers with leaves and twigs in their hair. When they were exterminated, all of civilization would be better.

The dusty trio fell into the road from the desert scrubland and began to ascend the small rise. To his left, near the apex, were two large boulders as big as any cabin and providing an excellent screen for anyone waiting to waylay a poor old dirt-scratcher. He knew they were there; he could actually see them through the rock. He tensed as he approached and studied the rock so that he could make eye contact with whomever was there. Perhaps seeing him face to face very close would dissuade them. His heart beat so violently that he could feel it. It shook his chest and hurt his head as if it was going to bust. Coming abreast of the boulders, he could stand it no longer. He reached back and grabbed one of the Hawken rifles from the first mule. His furtive eyes searched frantically, but he could not make his gaze light on any particular spot.

There was nothing. His adrenaline flushed and he began to shake from weakness. This had happened before in western Carolina many times during the war as one side or another rode through his tiny farm, then frequently as he and Sarah made their way from Missouri to Oregon. Nothing had ever happened. The troops and brigands of the war never became hostile to him, even though many other settlers in the area had been shot or hanged. And the Sioux and Arapahos and others had threatened violence, but nothing had ever developed. Still, though, it wore on him. With each one of the countless events, he would become so taut that he thought of himself as a guitar string. And each release was just that, a release of his energy. And yet some energy remained, enough to where he felt the need to expend it. But there was no log to chop, no ditch to dig, nothing to dissipate the last pockets of the energy. So his body shook.

The Hawken was almost too much to carry, but he held onto it down the slope and into the yard, which was nothing more than a large dirt area denuded of shrubs and scrubby trees. He was not sure his legs would support his weight, but he kept moving. It felt good to do so. He staggered to the pump well and let the mules noisily drink their fill. The water looked brown tinted but well enough for the desert, so he dropped his hat in and returned the full crown to his head, letting the contents soak over him. The

Hawken was still across his lap. A noise from the dirty adobe jacal drew his attention anew. A smooth-faced individual was studying him from a wood-framed window. There was discussion with an unseen person, and the window was suddenly empty. With a great roar, a bearded man burst from the jacal.

"Who are you? Why are you here?" The words were loud and angry. For emphasis he stabbed the air with a shotgun.

"Be kind, mister. Water in Arizona ought to be shared. I'm not after food or shelter."

"Well, it's not a crime to come up on two men, but it is damned bad manners. You too proud to give a 'hello the house'? Might save you gettin' shot some day!" Clearly the bearded man was not cooling off.

The would-be miner took a different approach. "There's Apache afoot—"

"There's always Apache around here!" interrupted the man. "This is goddamned Apache land and we're smack in it! Get your water and move on. No more than half an hour."

"Mister, I appreciate the hospitality of your camp. I do. But I have arrived at this destination by the grace of God and the skin of my teeth. Providence has delivered me, and I do not wish to turn my back on Providence. When I say there are Apaches afoot, I mean just that. Though I have not seen a sign of one, the..." He stopped to reconsider his words. "I reckon I have seen sign but no Indian. You see not one bird has flown around or near me this morning. They've been still. And a javelina ran through my camp. Now, nothing would make a pig scamper into my ground unless somethin' drove it." He looked around nervously and pointed his rifle at the higher rocky hills to the north and east. Was there movement?

CHAPTER 34

TUESDAY MORNING

As the white men talked, Ugly had drawn his bow and taken aim. Both the whites had long guns apparently in good working order, although the earth-scratcher had an older model that was less desirable. Serious Face, armed with a stone-headed club, and Walking Knife were behind the hacienda, trying to see the smooth-faced white man. Ugly did not see the need to observe. These whites did not speak Apache or, to his knowledge, Spanish. None of his band spoke English, though some White Mountain and Chiricahuas did. With no ability to communicate, it did not seem likely, in his opinion, that they would be able to discover why these whites acted as they did. What could Serious Face and this stranger hope to see by poking their heads in a window?

Just as he relaxed his bow to rest his arms, the earth-scratcher pointed his rifle in the direction of Ugly and the others. They had been seen! He let loose a quick shot and the others joined in. Tall Cactus, named because he was tall, almost as tall as a white man, had taken Serious Face's rifle and fired a shot. (Serious Face did not want the rifle to be lost to the group in case he was injured at the house.) More fired their bows, and at last everyone was involved.

Old Pete had been about to address possible movement when there was an exasperated gasp of air from behind him. For some reason his host would not calm down. The miner turned again to address him and to attempt to assuage the large, bearded man's frustration, but he drew short. The bearded man was on his knees, an arrow piercing his ribs and a bloody bubble at his mouth. Despite being battle ready just moments ago, he was now completely off guard. A rifle shot sounded from somewhere, and another arrow whizzed by his head. As his mind scrambled to develop a plan of action, there was a scream in the hacienda. Forgetting that he held a Hawken in his hands, he dropped it and raced to the mule to fetch the second rifle, then stopped midway to reach back for the first rifle again. As he picked it up, a bullet hit his forearm and he collapsed to the ground. The arm bent back at an angle and he knew he was useless, and therefore dead. In some absurdity it calmed him. There were no intimidating yells or dog-like yips. Only a succession of arrows until several found their mark. Then, from his view in the dirt, he saw several brown figures emerge carrying knives and stone-headed clubs. If there were more screams from the house, he was oblivious to them.

The next moments were a curiosity to a young but experienced warrior like Walking Knife. Ugly was well pleased, and Red Buffalo Calf seemed to have vented his anger and frustration and fear, showing such brutality that all were satisfied. True, all had participated except for Serious Face and Walking Knife, but his Mescalero friend had shown special brutality. Only the captive in the dwelling remained, and he was well in hand. After much screaming and resistance, he had fainted, but he was revived several times to see what was happening to his friends. Now that it was all over, they could turn their attention to that one. Now the People would find out why white men would have sex with each other.

CHAPTER 35

TUESDAY AFTERNOON

Farrell O'Meara attempted to focus his bloodshot eyes on his Man Friday, but through deceit, lack of character, or alcohol, he was unable to. Bendix was sheepish, so each looked into the other's chest as they sat across the desk in the office of the Nantucket Whaler.

"Well, that goddamned Greybib ran right off the rails. That was good money just pissed away. Three hundred dollars of badly needed capital, just pissed away."

Bendix shot upright. "Farrell, did I forget to tell you? I can't believe I missed that. Why, I told that old loafer the job was three hundred dollars upon completion. I only paid him two hundred fifty dollars, with the last fifty due when that son of a bitch Brody was out of town or dead." He reached into his pocket as if to fish for coins. "Nope, it must be in my cabin."

O'Meara finally looked into Bendix's face, and he looked as if he smelled bad fish. He did not trust the man any farther than he could throw him. If a man would lie, cheat, and steal from one, then he would lie, cheat, and steal from all, period. And he knew not to count on this sycophant to act honorably, for O'Meara certainly did not plan on acting honorably himself. The question at hand was why this was just now being brought to his attention, two days after the fact. He watched his confederate and supposed confidant struggle in the silence. He decided to wait it out. He would make Bendix crack.

O'Meara did not shift his gaze. He waited for his opposition to melt or own up to what he supposed was a foul deed. Bendix had committed some shenanigan with the money. He was sure of it. It was the alcohol, that was all. The drink kept him from following the natural progression of malfeasance, but if he just kept his own mouth shut, that fat pissant would stew in his own lie and spill over himself. There was no way, absolutely no way, that Bendix was going to outsmart him in any endeavor.

"Yeah," the man continued, somewhat shaky and uncertain. "I guess after what happened, and with getting that wagon to Tumulca, I just forgot about it. Sure did. But I'll go and get you that money, don't you worry, boss. I'll get it today."

O'Meara continued to glare. After several more seconds passed, he decided to respond.

"Mighty odd, you."

"What do you mean, boss?"

"I mean that amount," O'Meara fired back. "What's the idea of taking it upon yourself to negotiate a deal? But mainly, see, I'm curious about that amount. If you had given a third or a half, well, that's business. But you holding back that last fifty? Well, see, that just strikes me as curious."

Bendix looked incredulous, or at least made the attempt, though O'Meara was pretty sure which. "Well, I am sure I thought he wouldn't do that kind of work for less. That..." He hesitated. "That amount was just a small bonus."

The owner of Fuerte Viejo slowly stood up and supported himself with fists on the table. The room swayed just momentarily with the influence of the alcohol he had imbibed. Once everything righted itself, he spoke slowly and deliberately. "See here, you. You are not to ever take it upon yourself to interfere with me again. You do what I tell you and not one thing else. Do you understand me?"

"That ain't fair, boss. You know it! Why, I was only trying to help you. I saved you fifty dollars!"

"Get out now. And you bring me back that fifty dollars like your feet are on fire."

Bendix removed himself without speaking. He sauntered down the steps and through the barroom. He cursed the old Yankee and then himself for almost blowing it. He quickly entered his cabin and went to the barrel stool that served as his chair for visitors. He pulled out the ten ten-dollar gold pieces that were part of the original payment for Greybib. While it was true he had held back fifty dollars for the boss in an attempt to ingratiate himself, he had also held onto fifty for his own troubles. A man had to make it any way he could, he had reasoned at the time. But somehow the old Yankee had caught wind of it. No, it was probably just natural suspicion. And now, instead of being more trusted than ever, he had become suspect. Damn. Damn it all. At least the town constable was ignorant of his participation in the Greybib matter. Of that he was sure. Certain. Because if Brody did know, he would be dead right now. Bendix swallowed hard at the thought.

CHAPTER 36

WEDNESDAY MORNING

Even from a good rock's throw away, Johnny Wheeler could hear the rhythmic creaking of Miss Sarah's bed. He was not supposed to call her Miss Sarah, or Big Sarah, or refer to her in any way. As far as his ma was concerned, the pretty lady did not exist at all, and she expected her eleven-year-old son to ignore her as well. But it was hard for a boy to be oblivious to *that* woman. He could no more ignore her than he could ignore a paddle-wheeler back home, or a Gila monster or a jar of Micah's rock candy here in Fuerte Viejo. Miss Sarah was built to withstand a hard squall, he had heard an old miner say. And keeping an eye on her was much more fun and educational than sitting in front of the Nantucket Whaler saloon.

Johnny considered himself a very lucky boy, or almost a man, for he had seen it all. Though she kept a broad calico cloth hanging in her window as a curtain, it never reached from side to side. It was an easy way to spy at night, but he was too smart to use that ploy during the day. No, he reckoned the small bit of Cherokee in him told him that peering in a window would cause his body to block the afternoon or evening sun and cast a shadow into the little house, thereby drawing her attention. Also, he could be very much out in the open and obvious to any of the other people who happened by in back of the row houses. He reasoned that if caught, he would be in for a good thrashing from whoever caught him, another from Miss Sarah, and finally his ma and pa would beat him to a fare-ye-well. So he knew to crawl low and peer in where a sunken floorboard had pulled from the wall. From his vantage point, he had observed the object of his prurient curiosity on four separate occasions and, at least in his own mind, had become something of a man.

For the moment Johnny was disappointed to see that the new man, Mr. McLeroy Banks, was on top of Miss Sarah, but there was still a tantalizing bare white leg and foot waving wildly in the air. There was the familiar twitching in his pants, and he now was faced with a tightness that was all but unbearable. While his right hand worked to stifle his erection, the left attempted to widen the gap in the floor with a gentle tug.

Without so much as a groan of warning, the timber snapped with the bang of what sounded to the guilt-ridden eleven-year-old like a huge pine falling in the forest. The creaking of the bed continued unabated, but Johnny, sensing Banks's big hand pulling him through the hole, rolled away from the house and clumsily struggled to get to his feet, kicking up clouds of gray dust with his crusty leather shoes. He kept one hand on his hat as he pumped the air and gained momentum with the other. He hurdled a tin bucket that lay on its side and then a wooden one that was upright. Gasping for breath from fright and shock rather than from exertion, he exited the cleared yard and reached the relative safety of the desert itself. Still motivated by fear and not as yet able to ascertain the outcome, he continued his frantic pace. Were Mr. Banks and Miss Sarah right behind him?

He rounded a compass barrel cactus and a green wooded paloverde. As he swung around a giant saguaro, he ran right into the most obese Mexican he had ever seen. The man was very solid, and before Johnny bounced off and crashed to the ground, the man grabbed him by the arm and held him upright.

"Ah, ah, ah," the man said, wagging a finger. "You bad, *niño*. We going to be good friends, you and me." And the man tightened his substantial grip.

Minutes later Johnny sat on the ground, dumbfounded. He did not want to die, not yet, but he felt very dirty and immensely ashamed. He felt so dirty that he did not want to feel his own skin. The fat man grinned. "We be back soon, but you no talk. We Hombres be back. You no talk or you no see you mama and papa no more." He laughed as he tilted his hat and picked up a shiny brass Winchester repeater. But Johnny could not look at the man or the rifle. He could only sit and stare at something that must have been miles away, if it was even there at all.

CHAPTER 37

WEDNESDAY MORNING

Old Micah stood on the shaded veranda of his store and seethed. These days it did not take much to get him angry. When the white prospectors returned to town from their five-, seven-, or nine-day outings, there were two places that would normally demand a first stop. One was his store so that he could assay the ore and give a fair price, or something close to a fair price. Also he had the tools, should they have to replace any that were broken or lost in the desert. But if the ore was pure enough, judged by sight alone, then the first stop would be the Nantucket Whaler. There Farrell, dear cousin Farrell, would exchange the ore for alcohol and a meal. One way or the other, the O'Mearas would have the town sewn up. Micah was known only as Micah, no last name, and as such everyone was ignorant of his family tie. It was easy to pass off, as there was little open communication or familiarity between him and his cousin. And almost any was too much to suit the old storekeeper.

After years in San Francisco, running every kind of business, legal and otherwise, Farrell had left the Barbary Coast to investigate mining in Arizona. What he had told Micah was that an unsettled and unspoiled mineral paradise lay outside of Santa Ynez. While the Apaches had kept the Spaniards and Mexicans at bay, the whites would flood the territory now that the war was over. The two cousins would make their fortune mining the miners by selling land lots, picks and shovels, and arsenic and alcohol. That was Farrell's promise. Instead Micah had found a land of furnace-like heat and scant deposits. Nothing assayed for more than a few cents a ton. There were hostile Indians on every front, and the cavalry was not handling the situation to his liking. And whatever he tried to bring by way of freight from El Paso was pirated away by Los Hombres. The pot of gold was simply a stone cairn.

So his normal anger and sourness were now magnified by the prospectors' breach of protocol. They were at the end of the street across from that Jezebel trash, Verly Harvill. To be sure, she made men's shirts and pants, as well as dresses, but why should she get their business first? Where did they get the vital cash needed to pay for such items? Maybe she was selling flesh. She had the look. No decent woman would be here in the territory alone, anyway. He shook his head and clucked his tongue at the thought of it. If Farrell was going to send riches his way, he had better do it soon.

CHAPTER 38

WEDNESDAY MORNING

Brody and Peter Heydt had been sitting on the bench on the side of Haslett Brothers for close to half an hour and without a word being spoken past the initial greeting. Both had removed their hats to receive the warmth of the new day, but the hour was such that the heat was already rising, and they would have to retire indoors very soon. Through half-closed eyes, Heydt watched the stream of prospectors and rock hunters coming into town from north and west. Brody was more fidgety, shifting from one hip to the other and rubbing his hands over his face in a vain attempt to wipe away the nervousness. They watched the anxious inter-action between the returning men struggling in from the harsh desert environs. There was much hailing of one party to anoth-er. Everyone asked if there was any luck for the other. As always there were no definitive answers, only "we'll see" or "only the as-say will tell." But there was a congregation up the street opposite Verly's that held Brody's attention. Quickly, with a purpose, two men from the gathering strode toward him. He knew their faces but not their names; although he had already been introduced to them, he could never retain names. So much time had passed now that it was too awkward to inquire. They made their way toward him and it was obvious that he was the object of their destination. To let them know that he was aware and receptive, he replaced his hat and stood.

"Something's happened?"

"Yes, sir," said one, looking down the street to avoid eye contact. "The thing is...we are pretty sure something has happened. Yep, pretty sure." He looked at Brody at last. "We've been out past the McCords' place, us two and Old Pete. A little to the northwest, we was working an arroyo that has a lot of black sand, one that runs out of the Candelaria Mountains. We didn't think it was safe to go farther into the mountains, but Old Pete wanted to have a look. He took two mules and disappeared. That was just two days ago. He just wanted to dare a look-see before we headed back to town. He never came back and he ain't in town now."

"Okay," Brody said. "That sounds like something bad, but could be he just fell and hurt himself. Maybe even he found a lode and has started to work it."

"No, sir," said the other man earnestly. "Yesterday we were coming back, about four miles or so west of the McCords', and we saw a lot of smoke. A lot. Could only have been a fire like an Indian attack, like the whole place was blazing. That could only be Indians. The smoke was as black as it could be. Well, Old Pete would have come back that way if...well, no, he would have just had to come back by that way. It was close to the road going from the Maricopa Tanks. Truth is, we expect the worse."

"Yeah," said Brody with reluctance. "That doesn't sound good at all. I suspect y'all are right, though I hate the thought of it." He looked down at Heydt, who was still sitting. "You in any mood to take a look? Maybe there is a survivor. Maybe it's not too late to do something."

"Of course, Edwin. Just let me gear up. Probably need to send a rider to the fort to get some official help. And maybe Chief Juan Black Shoe too. You know, as a tracker."

"It could have been us, you know," continued the first prospector. "We just followed the arroyo west instead of east. If not, we would have been on the road too. "

Brody knew they were looking for comfort, for some justification of their own lives. He understood their need but did not know how to express his thoughts. Maybe he did not have any thoughts to give. Without a word he strode to the jail to fetch his blanket, haversack, and powder and lead. He also thought he would take every canteen he had and then get some more from Micah. If he left town at once, he would probably be back early tomorrow if all went well. But he slowed with the realization that there were two things that needed to be done. The first he would address now. He came to a dead stop, then reversed himself to go back from the jail and across to Micah's. The old man retreated to the interior of the store, either in fear of Brody or in anticipation of a sale. Brody moved quickly up the wooden steps. It occurred to him that he did have a reply for the poor mining duo, so he hollered over to the trio at Haslett's. "You're alive. Don't make any apology for it." It came out more harshly than he'd intended, but it could not be taken back. He gently opened the door with the tip of his boot. He gave Micah a brief nod and strode over to a table where lay a brown leather belt and two holsters. Contained within were two cap-and-ball revolvers, Colt Navies, modified to fit cartridges. He had seen them before, but they were something to be admired, not actually purchased. Today he would take them.

"You don't have money for those," said Old Micah rather meanly.

"No, but Farrell O'Meara does, and you will put them on his account." He gave the old New Englander an absolutely blank face, as if they were discussing something as mundane as the color of the sky. "You'll do that now." He continued to stare until Micah turned away. The old man grabbed a pencil and began scribbling on his countertop, presumably a bill of sale or invoice for the town patriarch.

Chore number two Brody was not quite prepared to address. However, it must be done. He wrapped the gun belt around his waist as he made his way to Beverly Harvill's Dress Shoppe. The sun continued to beat a tattoo upon him, but his mind was clear and sharp and right.

CHAPTER 39

WEDNESDAY NOON

"So you're going to leave, then?" she said pointedly.

"Verly, you know I must. We're probably too late to help, but I must be able to tell Big Sarah what, if anything, has happened to Old Pete. She deserves an answer."

"I ain't saying you're wrong. Not saying that at all. But what if something happens to all of you? What about all of us if we lose you and dear Pete Heydt? That's selfish, I know, but Mr. Banks seems capable. Maybe he and that professor can take the Papagos up there and find out what happened."

He pleaded with his eyes. How could he make her understand what she must surely already know? How could he make her understand duty when nobody had ever shown duty and devotion to her? Only that policeman in St. Louis, and he had died for it. Brody did not want to go and certainly did not want to hurt her. As to his own death, he did not care.

"I cannot send others to do my job, to do my duty. If something has to be done, something bad, then it falls on me, and I am the only one to face it." He looked down at his feet. "I have killed. So it may be that I have to do it again. It's not fair to put that burden on others."

"Is that what you want? To kill? To add to your burden?"

"That's not it. Do you think killing is what I enjoy? How can you? My heart was born hurting, even before I ever killed that cur in El Paso. Like Cain in the Bible, I carry a mark, a mark since birth, but it is on the inside of me. It is a stain that is inside me. How could you ever think that such a harsh thing gives me joy? I am a damned man—I mean a man that is damned—and I would not dare put that on anyone else. Not ever."

She sat down. "I am so sorry, Edwin. It is not fair of me. I knew it was wrong when I said it. Please forgive me. But will you at least talk to me and tell me so that you can die in peace if you must? Let me know what hurts you so, what you have done to carry so much guilt." She seemed to sigh. "Clean your conscience, please."

Brody took one knee beside her. "Today I actually feel well. Maybe having a purpose helps. But today is different. You've seen me. Most days it's bad, real bad."

"Yes, Edwin, but tell me why!" She threw her hands up in frustration.

He sighed heavily and clenched a fist to his head. His hair was too short to pull. "My head just won't be right! It's anguish all the time. I know that bad things are going to happen. I don't know what these bad things are, I have never known, but there is a sense of dread in me all the time. Nothing can give me joy because I know it is all short, it is all temporary. The bad things are always around the corner."

"You mean you get a premonition? You can see what happens before it happens? Or do you mean monsters?" She clasped his hand in comfort. "You are doing real good. Just let it out."

He shook his head. "No, no, no! It's nothing real, nothing like a killing or a fire where I can say that I imagined it before it happened. It is not as if I am some spiritualist or seer from the Bible."

He paused to stand and then took some paces, collecting his thoughts and working his fists against each other. "Miss Verly, this dread…this dread that I have every day…I just cannot describe it. The words are not in me. But there is no joy because I know that any time—<u>any time</u>—something can tear it all away, some bad thing that you are not even aware of. Perhaps I can describe it. When I wear my hat, there is a darkness over my head. There's a blackness that is present, but I don't really stay aware of it. But this is like wearing a hat all of the time. I don't see it, not really, but it is there, just out of reach of my eyes. When I have this sadness, this despair, all my energy is gone and the darkness is all around me. It is above and below and all over. It has never occurred to me before, but it must be like wearing a veil. It is a veil so fine you can see through it. Or maybe it is like looking through brown glass. It is so real. And this veil carries weight. It ties down my whole body. I shrug and twitch but it won't come off of me."

She stood too and grasped his hands to pull him closer. "Honey, that is terrible. You cannot live like that."

"I know, Verly. I live in defeat. Before the war, since my child days, I knew if I was to have a house, a spark from the fireplace would burn it down. If I was to purchase a wagon for freighting, the axle would break and the goods would be lost. If there was a sack of gold eagles on the table, someone would come and steal it. I just cannot allow myself to win. There is no pleasure to be had. And of course the war just made it that much worse. I have seen devastation and ruin—my home, yours, everything around me gone or taken. I just cannot get happy."

"Do you pray?"

"It helps, but only for a while. There's more to it than that, but maybe we can discuss that later. I do not think that you can stand to hear it all at once. But it tires me, Verly. It exhausts me. There is just no strength in me. Sleep is my only relief. I go to bed so early sometimes it is still light, and there is no sleep to be had. And I drink to make myself sleepy, or to make me so dull that I'm indifferent to that veil. But seeing you helps, it does. I get a feeling when

I see you, like the sensation of drinking water when you're thirsty. Seeing you is refreshing, like a breeze."

"Edwin, aren't you afraid I will leave? What will happen to you then? And aren't you afraid of dying out there?"

He looked at her with a wry smile. "If you leave me, then I have had the pleasure of knowing you. And I presume I will have your memory and a hope for correspondence. There are the mails. And if I should pass today…" The smile faded. "If I should pass, then my relief will have come. And before I die, I will have known you and gathered some strength from your presence, and from knowing that you faced hardship and licked it."

Her tears came at that point, just as his had come days earlier. She took quick steps and buried her head in his chest. "Go, Edwin Brody. Do your duty and be careful. Be very careful and come back to me."

He raised her chin and kissed her for the first time.

CHAPTER 40

WEDNESDAY NOON

B rody saw Professor Metz astride a big bay and shook his head firmly. "Sir, this will not be a picnic outing. Please dismount and return to the hotel. I'll not be responsible for your death."

"I will not be a burden, Mr. Brody. And as I have had some exposure to the medical arts, I may be of some benefit to you and the others. It may prove to be a boon to have someone such as myself aboard this venture. And if I am to learn—"

"Whatever," Brody interrupted. "If shooting starts, hunker down behind a rock or let the horse take the road. He'll know his way home, by and by."

Chief Juan Zapata Negro gave a high-pitched laugh and gave the professor a hearty slap on the back. "He friend of Juan. Juan keep safe, you bet. You see. Him no die today, you bet."

The town lawman paid no attention to the chief. His mind was elsewhere, going over each member of the party, which for some inexplicable reason was lined up facing south. Brody looked each member in the eye to ascertain who was capable and who should be left behind. There were four Anglos other than himself—Spencer, Banks, Heydt, and Metz. There was the checker-playing Mexican, Felipe Lopez, who could speak Apache, as he had lived as a captive for several years as a child. And there were four Papagos, including Chief Juan and his son Pedro. Brody pulled up on the two-gun holster to adjust its sliding weight. It was not a feel he was accustomed to, but he did like the way two pistols fit, as opposed to just one. He liked symmetry.

"Everybody got water to spare? Ball and cartridges? Spence, you got cartridges?"

The normally talkative Spencer merely raised a small leather sack and rattled it. Brody nodded but kept his eyes on the man. He had been quiet and reserved since the incident with Greybib Calhoun. Nobody was sure if it was embarrassment or physical pain. All had good sense not to ask. A man's emotions were his own, and it would be rude and imprudent to interfere. If Spencer felt like opening up, if he felt like revealing himself at all, then he would do it at his own choosing and most likely with Big Sarah, Verly Harvill, or any of the few bored housewives, like Mrs. Wheeler. And too, if he'd survived the war and all that entailed, then weathering one scrape on the frontier should not—*would* not, they reasoned— break Spencer.

He pulled himself up and into the saddle when a female voice hollered, "Wait, Wait!"

He turned to see an obese Indian woman helping an older black man off the boardwalk and into the dusty street. It was Old Abraham's wife, bringing him out to say good-bye to the posse.

"Old Abraham, you've too many years for this adventure. It says so right in your name."

"No, sir. The fire has plumb gone out of me, and my eyes ain't what they should be, no, sir." He looked up at the town constable with eyes cloudy and gray from cataracts. "But I wanted to do my part to protect the town. That's right, Old Abraham pulls his weight and does his due. I made some corn pones, and there is some dried antelope meat. It ain't no good to me, but my wife's family puts stock in it."

"We thank you, Abraham." Brody took the canvas bag. As each rode past, they thanked the old man for his concern and donation to their welfare. Brody led the line of men out into the wide street to turn them north. The men and women of Fuerte Viejo, the best throng that the feeble town could muster, waved and gave quiet but firm good-byes. And the last, a petite young blonde with a patina of makeup, stood at her doorway and rested her back against the frame, vowing not to cry again.

CHAPTER 41

WEDNESDAY AFTERNOON

Juan Black Shoe's son Pedro had been the first to see the vultures circling the McCord homestead. All four of the Papagos saw them, or claimed to have seen them, before the whites could confirm the presence of the large scavengers. And when the party of curious adventurers was close, those same four warriors declined the opportunity to inspect further. They had been asked to guide Brody and the others, and to offer their opinions, not to expose themselves to the ghosts of those who had fallen. Each was a Catholic, but Felipe, who was Mexican, explained to the whites that the tribal practices were still ingrained and that old traditions died hard. Even Christians, he said, believed in ghosts.

"Juan Zapato Negro, he has no dance to make white ghosts go away," Felipe said. "Papago family die and not come back. They think maybe dead white men come again." So the four Indians remained behind in a semicircle and rode a small distance from each other. They provided a protective arc while Brody and Banks and the others rode to a scene that none of them would forget.

The smell of smoke lingered in the air despite the length of time that had passed. No wind or rain had dissipated the pungent aroma of burnt wood and flesh. The sound of buzzing flies took them to a lone figure in the yard. A large man, obviously Lucas McCord, lay on his back with wounds too numerous to document. He had been pierced with many arrows, and a larger lance wound marred his chest. After death, or at least after most of the wounds, his shirt had been torn away. Banks determined this by the blood-stiffened shirt lying nearby. It lay flat enough to determine that holes on it matched or seemed to match the holes on the bigger McCord brother. The rust-colored ground was black with his thickened and dried blood. It seemed likely that he had died on the spot.

While the others examined the body, Felipe pointed to the blackened body of a man tied upside down to a wooden fence. He had not been totally consumed by fire, but his body was charred and disfigured where it had been pierced by several arrows and then lit. Much brush had been piled underneath him and set afire. They could not tell if the body was twisted in agony or from the effects of the fire contracting some muscles, but they did discern that great amounts of fat had burst from the pockets and run down the body and pooled on the brush. There was as much fat from this man as blood from the other.

While others whispered a word or two, Banks was the first to speak. "Thank God the papers never report more than just the death and some discreet violation. They don't paint the real picture, and I don't think the people could stand it if they did. They would call for the extermination of all Indians, not just the hostiles."

"Is this normal?" asked Professor Metz, holding a blue-dotted handkerchief over his mouth and nose. "Why such brutality? Why not kill your enemy and be done?" He stopped to wipe down his spectacles and then his face. "I do not fathom this brutality, this... this desecration. What level of hate these people must reach." He was clearly strained.

"Well, this is just typical, Professor," answered Peter Heydt. He cast the big Henry over his shoulder, for there was no more danger. "I don't think we've ever seen anyone just plainly killed by an Apache. Nope. They got to mutilate the body, tear it up like such. Could be they're really hateful, like you said, or it could be that they don't want the ghosts to come after them. Maybe they think that cuttin' up the man will make him just as so in the here-after. Chief Juan or his son Pedro can tell you. And Felipe certainly knows. I bet they all know. I think all tribes do it, from Sioux to Comanche to Apache. But hate is as good a reason as any. These people have been hunted and scalped, or hunted for scalps, and that might have caused what we see here. This may just be hateful revenge."

"So this is the two McCords?" asked Banks.

"No." Spencer finally spoke. "This is clearly Old Pete. I am afraid we still have one more to find and bury. Heaven help us." He cast a glance skyward as if to ask assistance from a divine being, or from the vultures.

In a matter of minutes, they had exhausted the immediate area. Only the interior of the wrecked cabin remained. They all looked at each other in expectation or desperation, but Brody quietly resolved that as the lone lawman, it was somehow his duty. He started to draw one pistol as he neared the entrance, but realizing the futility and its clear lack of purpose and necessity, he holstered it. Three of the four walls were still standing, and the roof had collapsed on that one side. He ducked his head and entered, cringing in anticipation of what he knew was there. He gave a cursory glance and saw nothing but burnt wood and debris, Then he took a slower, more calculated study. There was not a third body. He exited and shrugged his shoulders at his companions.

"Nothing. Matt has been taken by the hostiles. Let's just bury these two and report to the fort. It's all we can do."

From farther out, Pedro hailed the group. "Behind you, Mister Edwin. There is another body behind you in the brush."

Peter took a few steps around the squat ruin and confirmed what Pedro had seen. "How in the hell did he see that?" he said, more to himself than to the others. He looked back at the Papago and could discern that the latter was mounted and on somewhat of a rise. However, it was still a remarkable feat to have seen the body. He waited for the others to catch up, and as a group they took a closer look at the corpse of Matt McCord. The figure was nude, the eyes glassy blue and open, as was the wildly twisted mouth. It was a garish leer, the stare of a maniac. The body was covered in dried, caked blood that had smeared across the chest, stomach, and thighs and had collected underneath. They allowed their eyes to travel up and down, but the crotch drew their reluctant attention.

"Oh my God," several whispered almost in unison. No one spoke again for several moments as Pete, Banks, and Brody stepped closer still and studied the body. As the constable raised his hands to shield further viewing, Peter turned to Metz and the Papagos. "Only body missing is Matt McCord's. And now we've got it. Only…" He hesitated. "Matt McCord was a woman. Ain't no doubt about it but she was a woman."

CHAPTER 42

WEDNESDAY LATE AFTERNOON

Hannah Wheeler dropped the shirt and contemplated if she had died and gone to hell. The iron was hot, the little two-room house was hot, and the whole Philistine village burned her eyes every time she walked outside. There were scorpions galore and furry tarantula spiders the size of her hand. There was no food and less water and not even a Christian church where she could go and pray for assistance. There was the Catholic mission across the street, but those people were not like the good Irish and European Catholics of Georgia. No, these were Mexicans and Indians, and she doubted that the O'Briens and the Duvaliers back east would drink from the same communion cup as these dirty people. Any decent and respectable families, ones of long aristocratic bloodlines, were over in Santa Ynez. But her husband, Thomas, had decided that here was home, so home was here. And she hated it.

Worse, though, even more devastating than the heat, was the damage to her vanity. A handsome woman, she had attracted a number of suitors in her day. But four months here had aged her ten years. She was getting deep lines, deep wrinkles, around her eyes and lips. It was not fair. And her teeth were loosening. She was coming apart.

And the absolute worst was what was happening to poor Johnny. There was no school, no other children to play with (no white children, anyway), and he was sick again today. Since he had come back from his morning meandering, he had done nothing but lie in bed, and she could not coax a word out of him. There was nothing visible, no clue as to ailment or treatment, so she did what she thought she had to do: she ironed and prayed.

"Dear Lord, please deliver me and mine from this place."

CHAPTER 43

WEDNESDAY EARLY EVENING

The sun in the western sky beat down unmercifully, as if Sun God was punishing them with his anger, Walking Knife thought reluctantly. If Red Buffalo Calf had been sullen earlier, it was now his turn. As the Arivaipa band had headed into the Candelarias to plunder some small mine workings on the north side of Santa Ynez, the two travelers had broken away to head back south as they had come. Hopefully they would meet some Chiricahuas, faithful cousins of the Red Paints, the Mimbrenos, and then go back to the east.

He decided to speak his mind. "It bothers me deeply that we killed that woman. That is not the way the People believe. Our customs may differ from band to band—our stories may differ, our dances differ—but to kill a captive woman who has surrendered... I cannot even speak of such a thing. Cochise or Nana or Vitorio would never allow it."

"You are right a little bit, my friend. Your words are a little bit truthful and cause me some pain and annoyance. But you are free from my guilt and the guilt of the Black Rock Arivaipa people. I do not think I will come here again. This land is hot all the time, and there is no water. The people here are strange, both our people and the white people. The Inde here are different from what I know. The white people are different from the white people I know. When I return to the cool mountains, I think I will stay there."

Walking Knife stomped ahead and did not respond. Red Buffalo Calf took notice of this.

"You do not speak? This is because I killed the white woman? None of us knew that she was a female. This was not known to us until it was too late. She had not surrendered as you think. How were we to know she was a woman? You were angry with me before because you did not think that I was hard enough to be a warrior. You thought me weak. You did not say these things, but they were known to me by your actions. These things were known to me because I have the gift to read minds. Your mind and conscience are known to me. Now I say *you* are weak. They were white men living in a land that is not theirs. They had water in Apacheria, yet Apaches had to ask for it and to use it. When have you chosen to walk away from fighting white people when the numbers favored us?"

Walking Knife tried unsuccessfully to stifle his anger. "That woman could have been a wife for a warrior who has lost his own. The People do not kill enemies who surrender. The People do not kill when there is no need. We do not kill women. That is our way and has always been our way." He was close to talking matters of religion, a topic he wanted to avoid, but it was too late.

Red Buffalo Calf began anew. "I told you that we did not know she was a woman! And why do you speak of spiritual things? I have never heard you speak of our holy figures or holy spirits. You carry no bag of pollen on your neck. You never talk of mountain spirits. You are an Inde when it suits you. Ugly said the white man lifted his rifle. The whites began the fight. Would you wait until one of our own was killed before you fought? If you have lost the ability to be a warrior, throw away your weapons. If you are no longer a warrior, go live with the Pimas and plant corn. If you are no longer a warrior, go live with the Moquis and make blankets."

Walking Knife stopped and picked up a fist-sized rock. "It has been told to me that you are no longer welcome in the camps of the Mescaleros. I kept this to myself because to speak of it would be rude. But now I can say it and see why it has been said. You are not a good warrior and you are not a good person.

"You wept that you wanted to go home. I will help you." He hurled the stone as far to the east as he could, far enough that its landing was not audible. "The Mescaleros are that way. Go to them and do not bother me again."

CHAPTER 44

WEDNESDAY EARLY EVENING

I t was too late to start back to Fuerte Viejo, but the Papagos refused to camp where the murders had occurred—and that was what the group termed it, murder. The two McCord brothers (or were they husband and wife?) were buried side by side. Old Pete was given a spot some paces away, as if to allow the McCords some final modicum of privacy. As the Indians would not touch the bodies, all the work was done by Brody, Banks, and Professor Metz, with shovels provided by the deceased. Without a word of explanation, Spencer took his big-bore carbine and climbed the hill to provide guard. He had hardly spoken during the ride up, but when he saw and identified the wreckage of the third body, it was if he shut down altogether.

When the task of disposing of the bodies was completed, nobody felt like eating. The gruesome condition of the victims would be with them for some time. They all knew it without discussion. During the war they had been so hungry so often, almost continuously deprived of nourishment, that when food was found or rations obtained, they were consumed with little thought to conditions of the battlefield. Pork, fowl, and even corn were too valuable to be concerned over the appearance of a random arm, pool of blood, or the bloated carcass of a horse, or even the smell of the battlefield. But this was different. The shock and horror of a few years ago, while lasting, were subsiding, while this repugnant scene was fresh and new.

Poor Professor Metz, with his peripheral knowledge of the body and medical craft, was the most affected. He was distraught over the debasement of the female McCord. With eyes and face squinted, he asked again if this was normal treatment.

"Are women always raped and abused until death?"

"She wasn't raped," answered Felipe Lopez. "The Apache kill and torture, but, uh…" He struggled for the words. "I do not think there is even a word for it. It is not done, ever. It is hard for me to say from Apache to Spanish to American. But maybe it is what you call sin. Apaches do not take women to know them in that way."

The white men were not so sure, but Felipe had no reason to lie, and his word was trusted. There had been anecdotal evidence along the frontier, but always many miles away or years in the past. The famous Olive Oatman had disappeared and been held captive for years, but that had been the work of Mohave-Apaches scores of miles to the west.

"Professor," Peter Heydt explained. "It's just a horrible thing to say. It is. But the unwritten rule around here is to fight like the devil. If you holler and kill and fight with total abandon, and make your shots true, the Apaches may just back away. Maybe this is their respect for you as a warrior, or just because there have never been so many that they could weather the losses. I don't know. It's the only chance a man has, as to surrender is to suffer a death as you have seen here. But if the hard fight fails and you're sure to be overcome—why, then the last bullet is for yourself."

Somberly, Brody continued the lesson. "You see, Apaches kill everything and everybody. If they take a child, they may adopt it into their ranks, much as I've heard the Mexicans do with Apache children. Now, if they raid a Papago, Pima, or Mexican camp, they will take young girls and marry 'em. Those children and young girls will turn Apache just as if they had been born to it." He took

a swig from his canteen and almost gagged. The warm water sick-
ened him as he thought of the body fluids he had just been exposed
to. "I know Vitorio and some Warm Springs have caused devilment
over in New Mexico west of the Rio Grande. They're sure to have
murdered, but rape is something that the Apaches don't do. Felipe
could tell you more, but later. I'm tired of discussing it."

There was nothing left to say, and night would fall on them
during the ride back. So while Banks and Metz replenished the
canteens at the well, Brody went to gather Spence.

CHAPTER 45

WEDNESDAY NIGHT

The sun had kissed the horizon now and the sky had exploded into fantastic spills of orange and deep purple. The atmosphere among them was almost gray, a palpable gray that was near enough to touch, allowing sight for a little while longer. Unless he was asleep, there was no way that Spencer would have missed Brody's approach. The shuffling of gravel and heavy panting from the labor of the hike up the small hill belied the lawman's presence. Yet Spencer made not the slightest movement when his friend knelt beside him, though his eyes were open and looking northward.

"We're gearing up to head back. It's too late, of course, but Chief Juan and his boys are refusing to camp here." When there was no response, he continued. "We're filling up the canteens now."

Spencer finally spoke in an exhausted monotone. "Did you check the well to make sure there were no pieces of body floating in it?"

Brody leapt to his feet. "Well, by damned! Would they do that? They gotta use that water too. Goddamnit!"

"I don't know," said Spencer flatly. "Just seems like something we ought to check."

Brody placed his hands to the sides of his mouth to form a bullhorn. "Banks!" he bellowed. "Get a look at that water. See that it's safe." He delivered the words slowly to ensure their being understood. He knelt down again to address Spencer. "Come on, man. We've got to move." He tried to encourage more than admonish.

"It doesn't matter now, Mr. Constable. The Apaches are long gone from here, and we will not be attacked on the ride back. It is all over."

Brody paused. Spencer had never addressed him so formally. "Spence, I've heard they won't attack at night, but I've never trusted that supposed truth. Seems there is a rule that says rules are to be broken—"

"Nope," Spencer interrupted. "It's not likely, Edwin. Could be it's their religion that says they cannot find their way to heaven. Could be bullets are so hard to come by and arrows so hard to make that they don't want to waste them at night. But it's over."

Brody was losing his patience and his temper. "You keep repeating that it is over, yet I do not understand your meaning. You mean the fight is over? Please speak plainly."

It was several seconds before Spencer offered anything. "I mean the fight is over and it is over for me. I think I can find greener pastures in California or maybe Oregon. It probably doesn't burn like the furnaces of hell in Oregon."

"Spence, if you're embarrassed about that fight in the bar, it is senseless. Greybib doesn't fight fair and he thereby got the jump on you. I only won him out because I pulled my pistol before he was ready—even walked in with it out and cocked. You did not know to expect trouble, whereas I had been forewarned by that son of a bitch Bendix. It could've been me. Hell, it could have been Heydt or even Old Pete down there."

"No, it is more than that, Edwin. This place is so hot it gives me sickness. I'm tired of living where a man cannot catch his breath, where there are no jobs and no women. I would like to get married. I want to have a farm and a wife and children. I want to be cold sometimes without being sick. There is nothing here but heat and death."

Brody was exasperated but felt empathy. How could he turn his back on a friend, especially when this friend was as burdened as himself?

"Nothing you've said is a lie. Nothing you've said is wrong. I cannot argue with you because it is all fact. But we cannot keep starting over. This country allows a man many stops and starts. We've seen our poorest man elected president. You can climb as high as you want to go, depending on how hard you work and try. Some luck is involved too. But you cannot climb if you keep jumping off the ladder. We are losing our youth, and it is time that we walk a straight path."

There was a full half-minute of silence. Finally it was broken as they both looked straight ahead.

"There's more to it, Edwin. I..." He hesitated, and it was obvious that he was swallowing a lump in his throat. "I don't think there's such a thing as God. I'm not sure. It makes me a sad man. Please don't hate me for that. I cannot help what I do and do not believe." Then, as an afterthought, he said, "It makes me feel hollow. And it makes me feel ashamed."

Brody's reply was fast and shocking. "Well, you do or you don't. There is no middle ground. And why do you imagine I might hate you for that? Do you think I am that small-minded? Do you think I am one to judge the beliefs and morals of others while ignoring my own sins and shortcomings? You are a piece of work!"

Brody grabbed a rock and tossed it hard as his companion stared at him, eyes wide and jaw agape. "And another thing. If you don't believe in God here, you will not believe in him in California or Oregon or in the wilds of Canada. Running from an idea makes no more sense than trying to run from a freckle on your hand. My God, I thought you were smarter."

"Well, that's a comfort! Here I've been ashamed, and you treat me just as plain as if I never said anything about it. Thank you, Edwin."

"Good, Spence. Now will you mount your horse and prepare to ride? We will talk more, I promise."

As Spencer pushed himself up and cantered sideways down the slope, Brody added under his breath, "And brother, I may tell you the same thing. That God is pretty much a stranger to me as well."

CHAPTER 46

WEDNESDAY MIDNIGHT

The dying fire did nothing to penetrate the surrounding darkness of the desert. Without making too much of an effort, El Gato twisted his reclining figure to peer toward Midnight Sky and the other horses. As long as he remained motionless, the pain was slight or even nonexistent, but movement, even the gentle twist to his left, was excruciating. Piles. Yesterday he had reached back to examine himself and to his horror had found that there was seemingly more of him poking out than should even be inside him. When they neared a substantial town, maybe El Paso, he would have a doctor perform whatever magic doctors performed. But until that time, no one must know, for the men had to respect and fear their leader. The jefe must show no humanity, except perhaps those vestiges of lust inspired by a woman.

So when he grunted and winced to come to a standing position, the others looked on with fascination and, to no small extent, awe. Flacco, as short and skinny as a fence post, watched with averted eyes and nodded to two of the others. Each nodded to others until the whole circle was of bobbing heads like a yard of chickens. They tried to act as if nothing were out of the ordinary, but their awareness was obvious, since their normal course was to chatter like gossiping

139

women. But their attentiveness, curiosity, and violent nature led them to an incorrect conclusion. El Gato's stiff gait and grimace, they surmised, was from a wound suffered at the hands of the soldiers when the rifles were seized. A bullet wound, perhaps two, and without even crying out. What bravery and toughness! So El Gato's very human weakness, his frailty, only served to gain him more admiration.

He had left two men in charge of the horses. It was too early for them to be asleep, but if they were, the result of their laziness would be his knife in their hearts. To sleep on watch, to put one's needs above the survival of Los Hombres (actually his own survival was what mattered), must be punished by death. Examples had to be set. No one had questioned the death of that arrogant bastard Nuñez. Nuñez had jeopardized them all and his death had not brought the least protest, even from his cousin Gonzalez. Such were the rewards and expectations of being a bandit highwayman.

Fortunately, the men were awake. Though he could not see them in the darkness, they could discern his frame silhouetted by the fire. "Your horse, El Gato," they called out to him. "It is safe, of course. We would never let you down, boss."

"You are wise, my trusty friends, but know this: you guard all the horses not just for me, but for yourselves as well." It was a lie. "Your safety, your very life, depends on it." That part was true.

"Yes, boss, of course."

From farther in the darkness a voice hailed out, "Do not shoot me, you crazy fuckers. It is me, Gordito."

El Gato smiled and then erased the expression as he took a painful first step. "Come, Gordito. Tell me what is happening in that little gold mine of Fuerte Viejo."

"I have kept my eyes open, brother Gato. That village has whatever a man needs, you know?"

"Your needs are not mine, Gordito," said the bandit as his stomach turned ever so slightly at the thought of Gordito's perversions. "Tell me of the bank. Tell me what is there for my taking."

CHAPTER 47

LATE THURSDAY MORNING

It was close to dawn when they returned to Fuerte Viejo. Even so, light shown from inside the Sam Houston Saloon, the Nantucket Whaler, and one or two other homes and businesses. People were waiting for word of Old Pete and the McCords, not starting an early workday. Brody could make out a figure reclining in a chair in front of Verly's. She called out to him.

"What's the word, please, Edwin?" She rose and her black silhouette almost eclipsed the dim light from within her store. "Please tell me."

Before he could pull his horse over, Banks grabbed his arm. "It's okay. You do what you must and I'll speak to Sarah. I think she will do well hearing it from me."

Brody pulled away and whispered behind him, "Thank you, Mr. Banks."

"Then it is true," said Verly flatly. "I need to go with Mr. Banks. Sarah'll need me."

He slid off of his horse, weary and bone-tired, and slung the reins over the hitch. "She may need you and she may want to be alone. I guess you will know the answer, as women are gifted that way." He watched Felipe continue on down to his side of town with the Papagos in tow. She hugged him gently. "Edwin, may I get you anything? Coffee?"

"No, thank you, dear." It was the first time he had said it. There was no need to explain what they had seen and experienced. Verly Harvill had seen war and its horrors. She had been on the frontier long enough to know what bad news was. So they stood there and did not speak. They held hands and gazed at the sky and watched a thousand stars fade as the first intrusion of sunlight streaked its way westward.

CHAPTER 48

THURSDAY AFTERNOON

The day burned like no other. Everything seemed to radiate heat, even his arm when he held his hand to the cotton-covered extremity. To Brody the sun seemed to be an angry deity punishing its creation, and he wondered if the local Indians considered it so. Of course, the Papagos were Catholics now, or so Father Esteban believed, and Felipe and Chief Juan's son Pedro had said so. But they had never chiseled away the pagan rock carvings of spirals, deer, and other figures that littered the desert. Was there some modicum of ancient belief that was held in their hearts and practiced behind closed doors? Or were the old etchings allowed to remain out of respect for their ancestors? The whole thought process, and his conversation with Spence, left him uncomfortable and all too aware of his own religious shortcomings. There was the one Bad Thought that plagued him more than any other.

In the attempt to occupy his mind with other thoughts, he stood up from his chair in front of the jail and looked south, toward the ramshackle dwellings of the Indians and Mexicans. He was no longer forced to view the topmost portion of the chapel from this angle. And because he felt some relief from this, he felt guilty. He would have chuckled at the duality if he had been in better humor. But after a lifetime of such torment, and yesterday's murderous scene, all ability to smile was gone. He knew that Verly could make him feel better, but he hesitated. Perhaps, as she gave him strength, he would somehow weaken her. He wondered if there was some actual physical transference. And he could not yet bring himself to discuss religion with her. What if she was repulsed by his lack of religion and faith?

There were whites talking on the elevated porch of Micah's store, and here and there little brown children ran about chasing goats and chickens and each other. There was some energy to the town that was certainly out of the ordinary, and he wondered if Old Pete's death had given everyone something to talk about and reason to be out. Either the tragedy was a topic of conversation, or the townspeople felt the need to throw off the encumbrance of death by exerting themselves in social contact. He was certainly sorry for Big Sarah's loss, but he wished his regret would last. This sense of vitality and enthusiasm seemed to buoy him slightly, or at least to keep him from bottoming out and losing himself in drink or sleep.

Hearing some commotion from the south end of town, he watched Felipe make his way toward the jail. Despite the dust, his white pants and faded blue shirt looked immaculate. His brown leather sandals and feet, however, were almost gray. Brody stepped off of the boardwalk to meet him.

"Mister Edwin, my uncle comes from Sonoita. He says many ranchers are going west and north to Santa Ynez. Cochise and other Chiricahuas are busy there. He says some Pinals or Arivaipa are making trouble around Santa Ynez. The white soldiers ride around. Maybe they make the Apaches come this way. It is possible, yes?"

Selfishly, Brody thought of the trouble this would mean for him. Then, with guilt, he thought of the danger to Verly, Big Sarah, Mariana, and his Mexican friends and others. Ordinarily the Apaches, be they Pinal or Arivaipa from the north or Chiricahua from the south, would raid the fields but leave the town itself alone.

Rarely were even livestock taken. This was assumed to be because the Apaches were aware of the tenuous nature of Fuerte Viejo, and that they were cognizant that if they raided too harshly, the town would disappear, and a source of food with it. Such was the case with many smaller villages in northern Sonora and Chihuahua. So bereft were these areas that southern Chiricahuas under Juh were striking as far south as Durango. But some of the oldest inhabitants remembered times when the town had been hit so hard that almost nothing was left, so who knew? Was it possible to fathom the depths of Apache reasoning? Would these Apaches, trapped between soldiers and Santa Ynez, be more vengeful and react more violently than normal? It was a sobering thought. He reached up and pinched the bridge of his nose with two fingers and closed his eyes, attempting to formulate a plan of action or defense. The town was swollen with the prospectors, so it would never be as safe as it was right now. Perhaps they would do well to scout southward for a few miles and, by show of presence, dissuade those hostiles from coming too close to Fuerte Viejo.

"Felipe!" he called too loudly, for the young Mexican had not yet left him. "Ask for Mr. Banks at the hotel, and if he's not there, knock on Miss Sarah's door. Tell him to meet me here. Then ask Chief Juan Zapata Negro if he will ride with me. It looks like the posse will have to ride again today."

"Yes, sir, Mister Edwin. And Mr. Banks is to come to the jail?"

"Yes, and thank you, Felipe."

The young man ran up the street with the required urgency, and Brody went inside his office. He wanted to focus on something to make his mind slow down. There was the latest map of the territory, set in pink, white, and yellow. Maps were good and had always fascinated him. He took in the wooden rifle rack with its meager contents: a Henry that did not function and that he could not afford to repair, his Enfield from the war, and his shotgun.

Looking around further brought his attention to the table (there was no need for a desk with drawers) and the bottle of bourbon acting as a paperweight. Eyeing the dark brown fluid made him salivate, and he knew that it would make him feel better, if only briefly. It would ease his mind and bring him temporary peace, but therein lay the problem. Temporary peace was followed by lasting remorse and guilt. This was truer now that Verly Harvill was willing to work with him and give him assistance. She could help him now, but he did not want to trouble her again so soon, especially since Miss Sarah needed her too. Further still, he wanted to show her that he did indeed have strength, and he did not want to disappoint her. He had approached her with no thought of romance, only salvation, but he recognized that their struggles were intertwined and that they shared some kinship, some common tie with their lives' experiences. And he loved her.

So he settled himself with the notion that he and the posse would ride south for a day or so, and perhaps that would calm his mind in one sense and invigorate it in another. And he realized that he could take some pride in avoiding the alcohol and in being a leader in forming the posse to ride south. Maybe he was improving. How, he pondered, could a man be so mixed up?

CHAPTER 49

THURSDAY AFTERNOON

The storm clouds from earlier in the week had bypassed the area and deposited their moisture in the lands to the north and east. So now, alone and in an unfamiliar environment, the Red Paint Apache was desperate for water. To make matters worse, there were blue-jacketed patrols visible on the horizons since he had passed through the mountains that separated the two towns. Were these patrols in response to the raid where Serious Face, Ugly, and Red Buffalo Calf had killed the earth-scratchers? Or were they in response to some raid by Cochise and his band? There was small doubt that the whites would blame Cochise for those deaths and any others. Once whites learned the name of a headman, he became responsible for every act that occurred within a week's ride. Such was the case in his previous visit with the Tontos, when Big Rump was thought to be ravaging the known world, regardless of Yavapai or Tonto guilt.

Despite Red Buffalo Calf's admonition, Walking Knife had received fine training as a warrior. He knew to go to high ground and look for greenery. Larger trees, oaks, and grasses meant water. But here, farther south of the desert, everything was green, and there was little vegetation larger than the knee-high grasses. What creek beds he had seen were dry and sandy. Each had been thoroughly investigated by white soldiers, he knew, as the tracks of shod horses came not only from different directions but on different days. That meant that the soldiers knew where water was, or should be, and that they might come again. He doubted that white people had knowledge of such matters, so he theorized that some tribe had sent warriors to act as scouts. There were tribes far to the west who were not known to him. Of course, there were the nasty Pimas and Papagos, who were probably very knowledgeable too. He hoped not, for they might be able to read his trail and lead the soldiers to him.

He knew that several days' walk to the west, there was a river that was good and constant. It also represented the extreme boundary of Apacheria, and he was more likely to find those same Pimas and Papagos, and an early death. It made him question his decision to forego a horse. Certainly there was more stealth in traveling on foot, but a horse would have had him home by now. Conversely, he might never have reached this far if he had been burdened with a horse.

With no Ussen to hear his prayer, the only salvation lay in finding Chiricahuas to the south and east. They were hospitable kinsmen and would assist him in his needs. But to his dismay, they were not making themselves known, and all he could find were trails of those shod horses, those of the blue-jacketed soldiers. Perhaps the great Cochise had taken his bands to the cooler mountains in Mexico. So he would keep climbing hills, keep a lookout for the enemy and his kinsmen, and drink deep from the creeks and pools of the Red Paint People, should he find his way home again.

CHAPTER 50

THURSDAY EVENING

Farrell O'Meara sat at his desk and contemplated his current situation. He preferred to plan ahead and count on success rather than rue previous decisions and regret his actions. But a lot had gone wrong as of late. Greybib had proven to be a bust, El Gato and Los Hombres had not been heard from, and now he knew that he could no longer count on Bendix. And if he could not count on Bendix, well, then he was in danger legally and, more importantly, physically. The federal marshal would certainly have something to say about that load of rifles. Even if they were "lost" on the Mexican side of the border, he would face a stretch in Yuma for selling them to wanted men. There was no doubt that the fat bastard would spill the beans if the federals threatened him with prison time. And if Bendix squealed to Brody about the assassination attempt, that would mean his death. Period.

His saliva had become so profuse that he needed to spit. That was the signal that he had taken too much rum. He had not really been aware of getting drunk, it had just happened. And it happened frequently as of late. The bottle, marked Old Barbados, was not quite empty; perhaps two more drinks remained. It was, however, his second bottle. He took it and poured the remnants on the floor. The liquid hitting the wood made him think of peeing. Some minutes ago he'd had the urge, but it had passed. Or had he already gone? "Damn!" he said aloud, though he was quite alone. "I am drunk." He placed his hand in his lap and felt the moisture.

The saliva pooled in his mouth and he spat again, slowly and methodically. The vomiting would come at any moment. But he would not be aware of it for some time. He collapsed on his desk and slept the nauseated and unrestful sleep that drunkards endured.

CHAPTER 51

THURSDAY EVENING

It was but a few miles before the Sonoran desert gave way to the rolling grasslands. It was greener but by no means lush, not by the standards of a Georgian, Texan, Wisconsin, or man from any other state the Anglo men were familiar with. There were still the ever-present prickly pears and yuccas about, and some random outcroppings of stone forming domed crests and shallow canyons, but these would have been called rolling hills and deep valleys farther east. And likewise the sun, the giver of life to southern farmers, seemed to be only half as far from the earth here, and its presence seemed more deadly than healthful and helpful.

To the surprise of the men from Fuerte Viejo, it was Chief Juan Zapata Negro who rode ahead and scouted the terrain. They had fully expected a chief to be above such ordinary and plebeian work, but he was game. It seemed that he even preferred to be first, and that he trusted his own eyes and instincts above all others. Also, he relished the important position and the attention it garnered. He certainly seemed to revel in being observed by white men and demanding their favor, but it could be to prove to his younger men that he was still a warrior and a man to be reckoned with. As they moved southward and slightly eastward he would ride back within sight and motion his arms in a brisk and awkward manner. His son Pedro would interpret these indications to the party: "White soldiers rode east," or "They came back to the west."

When they saw him riding back at a slow and easy gait, they knew that there was no emergency at hand. By the position of the sun, Brody, Banks, and Heydt all independently decided that the chief was calling it a day. They were a couple hundred yards from the base of the hill with a slow seep that had been without a formal name for so long (an oddity in such a place) that it was now called No Name Spring. Daylight remained but water was here. They still had to establish a camp and prepare a Spartan meal. Their energy was sapped, and there was no shame in calling it a day this early. The stop was not any indication of soft living, and it was a wonder that the professor had stayed in the saddle this long.

"Let's retire to the spring and set up camp," Brody seemingly ordered rather than suggested. "That is, if the spring exists. We can rest and start out early in the a.m."

There was no further conversation. While the town had suddenly become vibrant in the aftermath of the death of Old Pete and the McCords, the travelers had made the brief excursion with no more conversation than Pedro's explaining his father's hand signals. And Pedro now relayed Brody's words to the other Papagos. Without further ado they steered their mounts toward a cleft in the pale green hill to their left.

It was Professor Metz who broke the silence. "Pardon me, Mr. Brody, but is it not the custom in these environs to travel through the night and rest by day? Am I mistaken?"

Showing not one bit of exasperation, Brody turned in his saddle and slung one leg over the horn in order to make himself more comfortable. As Brody was a slender man, and somewhat thinned by alcohol use, his horse did not contest the change in ballast.

"That is very much on the nose, my good professor. However, we are attempting to find sign. We need daylight for that. Now, if we had already cut some Apache's trail and knew more or less where to head to, why then we would hole up during the day and use moonlight to pursue them. To old eyes like the chief's, moonlight is enough to follow an established sign. Understand?"

"Why, yes, yes I do. That is outside my area of expertise, and I am grateful for your experience and knowledge. It is good to learn one new fact of knowledge every day."

Brody turned and whispered to Heydt, "Can the son of a bitch not just say thank you?"

Heydt laughed in response. The professor did use each and every chance to deliver a wordy exchange. They very much respected the man's intellect and desire for learning. It said something that such a man was not content unless he was striving for total knowledge. But they also had a deep resentment for his verbose nature. And here, with a posse, it rode on Brody in a very difficult way. The older man, like the others, had been quiet most of the day, but Brody realized that quitting now and establishing a camp would require conversation and a more relaxed atmosphere. He quietly hoped he would have the patience to behave in a gentlemanly manner.

CHAPTER 52

THURSDAY EVENING

When the group reached the springs, they were disappointed to find that it no longer ran slowly but rather trickled down the slope, seeping into one spot before disappearing underground and then resurfacing again in an alternating fashion. The only sign of its rainy-season glory was a sandy trough. Banks, Metz, Spence, and Brody all dismounted and milled about to set up camp. Chief Juan Zapata Negro and the Papagos rode about on a short perimeter, making one last check for security and talking among themselves. Brody strode out to inquire as to the delay when Pedro rode forward.

"My father says it is not safe here. He wants us to ride out to the open land where we can see better." He shrugged, either to show indifference or to convey that he did not understand his father's reluctance.

Immediately the older warrior rode up to address them. "Little bit sign here. Little bit. Not safe. Not safe."

This was a new development. All day long they had seen nothing but the marks of shod cavalry horses. Now Chief Juan Black Shoe was asserting that something had changed, something had spooked him. Brody looked over his shoulder at the others and at the grassy hill that rose up from the earth. The yellow-and-gray trough of the spring looked like a scar to mar its beauty, though oddly, in this terrain the spring was the true site to be determined beautiful. Camping by water was smart. If one were besieged by Indians and the horses were lost to theft, one could still hope to hold out for a while if there were water. However, the spring was nearly dry and might give out at any time. Also, they were at the base of the hill and subject to rifle fire and arrows from above. Perhaps they were too vulnerable here. The chief was enough of a soldier or warrior to know that.

"Very good, Pedro. We will follow your father's wishes But in a few minutes. The horses and men can rest a bit and take on some water."

Felipe made eye contact with Brody and nodded his head toward the flatter grasslands. Together the duo stepped out from the others and made their way through the knee-high grass until the young Mexican knelt and examined the tracks of another shod horse. There was nothing unusual about it, as they had been crossing the trails of soldiers all day. There had been some discussion as to their supposed action.

"More tracks, Felipe? The yellow-legs are sure earning their pay this week, are they not?"

"Yes, Mister Edwin. There are many soldiers. But you need to see something else." He stood and removed his hat with its tall crown. The hot, arid atmosphere had dried the sweat into his hair and thusly glued it to his head. "Behind me is the hill. There are two big rocks. There is an Apache there. He is there for a while, maybe. He is alone, I think."

Brody had been on the frontier long enough to know that he should not look immediately. Like with any other wild animal— and that was the only way to describe an Apache—it was necessary to appear at ease and nonchalant to stave off any aggressive maneuver. Because of this he carefully scanned the horizon in all directions until he took in the grassy slopes that burst from the earth like fingers beneath a green blanket. He carefully studied them for a sign of movement or any irregular pattern near the two large rocks, but nothing belied the presence of a human. Even so, he trusted Felipe and did not question the young man's word and ability. Felipe's skills were highly regarded.

"Do you see him, Mister Edwin?"

"No, but I know you saw what you saw, Felipe. What do you recommend? What do you think?"

"I do not know. I think maybe he is alone from his friends. The soldiers are so many. Maybe he only one alive, maybe he hurt, or they go apart to make soldiers confused. It is hard to know."

"What if we were to approach him?"

Felipe looked stunned momentarily, then lapsed into a wry smile. "I think maybe a hurt Apache shoot. I think a very not-hurt Apache shoot. I live with these people three years. If you want to talk, Edwin, I go with you."

Edwin Brody smiled back. He rubbed his hands together vigorously to burn off his immediate burst of energy or anxiety. "Okay, my brave friend," he said with a deep sigh. "Let's go get this done."

Brody returned to his compatriots and found them lounging or milling restlessly around the camp, the horses having been put on a picket. Apparently Banks and Spencer had decided this was where the day ended, regardless of anyone else's wishes. Chief Juan Zapata Negro and his men had dismounted but were standing by their horses, ready to ride again for what they proposed was a better site. They had segregated themselves slightly on the basis of planning rather than race.

"Everyone listen. Chief, *usted tambien, por favor.* Nobody"—he tried to make sure that he met every man's eyes—"nobody is to move. Keep your firearm near, but do not touch it. We may have a visitor, *un visita.* Everyone hear me?"

The professor, for once, stood mute, while the others looked at each other and nodded. Banks, who was reclining on one elbow, cast his eyes to his pistols and the newly acquired Henry rifle, but he made no audible reply. In his mind's eye, he reached for them to determine the distance and speed needed to acquire them. Heydt did the same with his Henry.

Brody turned back to Felipe and nodded. The young Mexican cupped his hands to his mouth and called out in a language that bore no kinship to English or Spanish. To the Anglos it seemed heavy with *ch*, *tz*, and *k* sounds. Felipe repeated certain phrases in a pattern, but not in the sing-song way of the Chinese, and they felt as intrigued to watch him as to watch the hill for whomever he hailed. But when Juan Zapata Negro and the Papagos began to chatter and stir and point, all eyes moved to the hill. On a rock, right hand held high to signify what they thought meant "peace" or "no weapon," was a lone Apache warrior.

"Good God almighty," said Banks with much less emotion than the words implied. He might have been talking about the color of a horse, but the lack of tension in his voice contrasted deeply with his strained face. The professor began to scramble, but Brody held up both hands and demanded that he stop.

"But you must get him down here. I must speak with this man," the professor pleaded.

"Felipe, do you think you can get him down here?"

"He listen to me good. I see." And he rattled off more with his own hands held high. His right was open and his left alternated between indications of the group and motions toward the Apache. The Papago chief began to tremble in rage.

CHAPTER 53

THURSDAY EVENING

Walking Knife had been dozing at the seep and daydreaming of Antelope Under the Moon when he was startled by the approach of riders. He had no time to react before the group of strangers had come within earshot. Acting immediately on his impulse to run, he took note that the hill was grassy and did not offer the heavier foliage that would have concealed him in an attempt to flee. As before, he knew that a horse would have allowed him to get away quickly, but would also have caused him to be seen by the enemy. He was aware of the contradiction, but there was no metaphor in his culture for "double-edged sword." Therefore he stayed put. With the seep disappearing and reappearing sporadically as it made its way down the slope, he felt assured that the horsemen would not climb to his position. But some looked to be Bean Eaters, Papagos. That was bad.

He made some furtive observations in an attempt to ascertain the danger. He kept his movement to a minimum, because movement was what drew attention. It was unlikely, but a man might kneel in heavy woods or among the flora of the desert and not be noticed; but if he stood or otherwise made movement, then he invited attention. And here attention meant danger and, ultimately, death.

His study was interrupted by a call from below. "You in the rocks—if you are of the People, we will not harm you. If you are of the People, we want to talk to you. This will be a talk of peace. My name is Felipe, and I lived with the People. It will be good to talk, I think. Our headman here wants to talk to someone of the People. It is safe and for peace. Do not take the counsel of your fear. You must be brave to be here, and we respect that."

Walking Knife's heart turned icy cold with a fear he had never before experienced. This was not a contest he had chosen, where he and others might fight with better odds against earth-scratchers or wagon drivers. This was a dozen against one. He, like all of the Inde, lived the life of the hunter and the prey. A life could slip away any hour of any day, but that fact was faced bravely and without the morose and somber fretting that wasted the days of whites and Mexicans. But here, far from home and alone with the dreaded Bean Eaters who were allied with whites...this was death most certain. This was the end.

But he steadied himself and stood upon the boulder with the stance of a warrior, ramrod straight and with his right hand open. If they were honest and wanted to talk, he would meet with them. If not, if they were full of treachery, then he would show them what a brave warrior could do.

CHAPTER 54

THURSDAY EVENING

Sarah busied herself about the ramshackle abode and tried not to think of what life was going to become. Since kind McLeroy Banks had told her of Old Pete's death, she had occupied herself with cleaning that had long been neglected. Everything had been swept and the wooden floors soaked with brine water and vinegar. And her only friend, Verly, dearest Verly, had paid two Mexican youths to work the exterior with a steel brush and then apply fresh white paint purchased from Micah's store. Being busy helped, but it was not enough.

She sat on an overturned bucket and watched the sun on its way to kiss the horizon. Old Pete had not come to Fuerte Viejo for its beauty. In his mind it had been only one step closer to the end of the rainbow and a pot of gold, a fairy tale. But she had found it beautiful, with its multihued landscapes and plants that were nothing like she had ever seen. Yes, there had been a visual allure, but Sarah did not know if she could ever see it again, certainly not in the same light. The burning orange and rich purple of the sunset now signified loss, and sadness.

Then too, Old Pete did not represent love, not true love, but safety, security, and comfort. Theirs was a love born of companionship and not romance. He was to be mourned and his loss lamented, for now and always. But she would survive. She would not let this be the end of her. She vowed to be sad but to be strong, and to continue living.

"I love you, Old Pete. I do. But I'm not going to die in spirit before I die in body. You taught me one thing: to survive. And I will."

CHAPTER 55

THURSDAY EVENING

As the lone Apache figure walked slowly but confidently down the hill, the Papagos became incensed. As a group they mounted up and headed toward the flatlands, the chief and son holding back slightly. There was much yelling, and the chief in particular was in a frothing outrage. Pedro reached for an arm in a vain attempt to calm him, but his father swatted the restraining appendage away.

"You trick Juan. You lie. No good, no good!" There was a mask of hate on his face as he screamed at Brody. Had the distance not been so far, they would have seen spittle fly from his mouth. He rode off, trailing the other warriors. Pedro, seemingly not knowing what to do, raised his shoulders in bewilderment at the townsmen, then took off after the other Papagos.

Their leaving and the division in the camp, rather than deterring the Apache, seemed to give him vigor, and he strode more quickly and even with a touch of arrogance. His right hand was no longer held high. He moved without any sign of hesitation.

"Bueno." He knew little in the way of Spanish, but he knew this was a word of welcome or of something good. He assumed that everyone spoke it at some level or another. All the Chiricahuas spoke it, and this was their land.

"*Habla español?*" asked Brody and Felipe in unison. The Indian shook his head. The white man turned to the Mexican, who offered nothing but a shrug, then picked up a blood-red blanket and spread it on the grass.

"Tell him he is welcome to sit here. We want to know if there are other Apaches here or any others about. You know what to say."

Felipe began his monologue again, and the Indian sat on the red blanket.

CHAPTER 56

THURSDAY NIGHT/FRIDAY MORNING

Three of the whites were silent and held back while the leader, a small and thin man whom Felipe said was an enforcer of rules, was quite inquisitive and showed evident intellect and honesty. Felipe himself relayed that he had spent three years with the local band of Cochise, so he could be trusted. And if Felipe trusted this leader, this enforcer of rules, then the Apache decided that he could too. There was some comfort in knowing that white men surrendered their individuality to others, to a chosen leader. If this white leader said that there would be no deceit, then the others would hold themselves in check. That obedience was something no Apache headman could ever hope to have, except maybe Cochise or his own uncle's uncle, Mangas Colorado, who had already been killed back home. He knew he was safe as long as he made friends with this headman.

The white leader, through Felipe, asked about the locations of food, water, and other Apaches in the area. Felipe had the good grace to use the word Inde, meaning the People, rather than the term Apache, a foreign word meaning enemy. Walking Knife held lying in disdain but did not want to say too much. He admitted to having a hard time finding water, affirming that the heat of summer was drying up springs and seeps. There was another river farther west that they knew of too, but it was not in the direction he was going. As for others, he had seen some Black Rock Arivaipa, but he had left them because they wanted to be around Santinez. That place, he said, was not to his liking, and he wanted to go home. He did not know where they were now. And all that was true and they seemed satisfied.

As the others fidgeted and squirmed and tried not to stare at him in rudeness, Felipe leaned in close.

"My friend, just north of our village there were two people, white people, who lived in the desert. They had an adobe house and lived very much alone. One was a woman. They are dead. Did the Black Rock Arivaipa do this? I do not ask if you did it. I would not put you in a position where you must answer such a thing. I just want to know if the Arivaipa did this."

The Indian knew to expect a tough conversation, but this was like a punch to his stomach. He took a moment to collect himself. After a deep breath he answered.

"Felipe, I am impressed with your truthfulness. I have believed that honesty is something unknown to whites and Mexicans. This has made me learn something new, as if I were a young boy. Why do you want to know about the death of those people? It is a bad thing to speak of that. I do not wish to speak of things."

Felipe nodded and let it go. That had been all the answer he had needed.

Despite everyone being bone weary, the group spent a long and restless night. Professor Metz, Banks, Spencer, and Brody did not fully trust the Indian, suspecting that he himself was too fearful to fall asleep before cutting their throats. Therefore they fought the necessity of closing their increasingly heavy eyelids, fear just narrowly beating exhaustion. In order to insure his safety, Spencer volunteered to take watch the entire night, climbing to a perch near the Apache's original hiding spot. None of the Anglos doubted he would stay awake and do his duty, yet that knowledge did nothing to abate their anxiety.

Walking Knife too found sleep elusive. Why had Felipe asked about the attack on the two men and their woman? Did truth in white men disappear like the sun when night approached? Did their guarantee of safety change when night fell? He had not considered that before and it caused him great discomfort. He sat and spent the hours in contemplation of what might happen next.

CHAPTER 57

FRIDAY MORNING

There had been no alcohol to encumber their awakening, so Los Hombres rose with the sun. El Gato reflected pleasantly that nobody had questioned Nuñez's death, Gordito's scouting mission, or why they should raid the little village of Fuerte Viejo. He laughed at the thought of Nuñez's death in the broiling little canyon and how that was a strong deterrent to any questions. Still, with it being early summer, he knew that there must be some curiosity in their minds. Why go if no crops were ripe? "Let the small-minded peasants do the work, and we will do the harvest," he had said last summer, and he chuckled again. They had hit the town in October for food and again in January, though the latter raid was simply to let the villagers know that they could strike at any time, in order to demoralize the hapless and meager farmers and miners.

Los Hombres were greedy by nature and followers by custom. Both traits suited him as long as they did not get too greedy and follow someone else. That was why he did not share plans with his men. It would not be unheard of for a lieutenant in some other gang to say, "The leader wants to do this thing. It is so small, so we should do something big." Or "This thing is too dangerous and we will all be killed. Let's kill him and be done."

Those conversations had certainly taken place elsewhere, but not with him and not with Los Hombres. He could be sure of that, for he had told no one but Gordito of his new plan. Old Gordito, his friend of so many years, would not wreck his plans, or his spoils. Of this he was as sure as the sun stretching above the eastern horizon. After tomorrow, when they emptied Señor O'Meara of his money and Fuerte Viejo of any loot, Gordito was going to die just in case.

Too, why would the men leave him now? No other outlaw was good enough to arm his men with new Winchester repeating rifles. No, Los Hombres belonged to him and would belong to him for a long, long time.

CHAPTER 58

FRIDAY MORNING

Hannah Wheeler stood in the doorway of her cabin and swept the dust and dirt out into the desert from which it came. The desert not only began at the door but seemed to penetrate the interior of her tiny wooden home. If she were to omit one day of sweeping, she reckoned, the land would reclaim her part of it, and there would be no indication that the Wheeler family had ever existed. It saddened her greatly. But she flung the broom a little harder and continued with her duty. If her husband did not find something in the next thirty days, she was taking Johnny and heading east, back home. They had discussed it, but her argument had fallen on deaf ears. She had promised God that she would stand by her man and obey him, but not at the expense of their son. Certainly Johnny's welfare would be understood to God. Could she last thirty days?

Johnny was still sick and refused to get out of bed until she scolded him severely. She watched him now, across the street or plaza, sitting by one of the broken walls of the old mission. Several young Mexican children asked him to play, but she saw him shake his head, and the little brown ones moved on to their own games and shouts of fun. Johnny picked up a stick and angrily gouged it into the wall, attempting to destroy it with small but determined strikes. What was this about?

From the corner of her eye, she saw Father Esteban leaving the cabin of that whore Sarah. Big Sarah! How common and undignified could a woman be, even here in the wilds? Certainly Father Esteban was too pious and, she hoped, beyond the years of having a dalliance. No doubt he was just providing comfort to one of the flock. That would be his duty—and if anyone needed to have witness, it was her. But at this hour, he must have spent the night. She decided that Catholic priests were of a different breed than good Methodists. Then again, maybe it was Arizona.

She watched as he made his way through the maze of broken walls and to the one surviving room that served as the chapel. Suddenly Sarah was at her door with her arms held before her, offering something covered by a checkered cloth.

"Good morning, ma'am. I have come to share."

Hannah Wheeler was very much caught off guard. "Why, hello. Uh, good morning. How are you?" She cringed because it was such a ridiculous question to ask a woman who had just lost her husband.

"Mrs. Wheeler, I have been better. Sleep will not come to me, so I spent the night baking and cleaning the house, though I don't suppose you would know that it's clean. When I cannot sleep, I figure the good Lord wants me to do something so that I do not waste the hours. There is bread here if you want it, and a pie made of prickly pear. They are good if you are not too used to something from closer to home." She managed a smile.

Wheeler was taken aback. She had nothing to say to this woman, a woman who made her living from sin and flesh, tempting others into her world. But here she was reaching out in the kindest manner. They stood looking at each other in awkward silence when a thought suddenly came to Hannah. What did Jesus do to the sinners? Cast them out and harangue them? No. And why should she act differently?

"Thank you for thinking of us, Miss Sarah. Would you come in and share a piece of the pie with a cup of coffee?"

CHAPTER 59

FRIDAY MORNING

"Riders from the west. It looks like soldiers." It was Spence standing atop one of the gray boulders, pointing to the horizon. Heydt steadied the horses at the picket and glanced back at the Apache, who was talking in a hushed tone or series of grunts to the professor, through Felipe.

"Edwin, what are we going to do about him?" Heydt nodded at the camp visitor. "This is going to be more trouble than we wanted."

Brody stared at Heydt as if he had not heard the question. The stare lengthened to the point of the latter being uncomfortable before the lawman broke his gaze and hollered to Spence. "How much time do we got?"

"Just a few minutes, Edwin. They're riding hard." He paused. "I am sorry, Edwin. I was so busy studying the east and south. I'm sorry."

Heydt and Brody both knew it was not Spencer's fault. Common sense and location (they were on the extreme western end of Apacheria) dictated watching the south and east as Spence had done. No pioneer of any experience would have expected movement, white or red, from the area behind them. Further, they had not spelled Spence to keep him fresh, and they all knew better than to let a tired man spend the entire night on watch.

171

All now was to be quickness, with no room for error. He began to spit commands with a delivery that displayed a confidence he would not have known he possessed. It was a confidence that made others obey.

"Felipe, get that Indian up there in those rocks and tell him to stay put. His life depends on it. Spence, you get down here. And you haven't seen those riders, understand? They are going to surprise us."

He then rushed to Heydt to help steady the horses. "It helps that we don't have an extra horse that we would have to explain. That is a blessing."

"Edwin, look!" Pete hissed. "This is getting worse. That's the chief and more Papagos. They led the cavalry here. We have murdered that Indian."

"Not yet, Heydt. I will not lie. They will ask and I will say he was here, but that I don't see him now." In his heart he sensed that it was futile, as was everything, but he continued like always.

A column of twelve men in dusty and soiled blue blouses rode in and stopped at the periphery of the camp, spreading in an arc around its perimeter, boxing the Fuerte Viejo men against the high ridge. With them was a young, thin man with skin so black that at a distance he appeared featureless. Another civilian was present, middle-aged and a trapper by his looks, with brown skin that looked like a dirty paper sack that had been repeatedly crumpled and smoothed back out. The crevices and wrinkles were a sign that the man lived in the elements.

"Gentlemen, I am Lieutenant Krieg of the Third US Cavalry. I would—"

"We are leaving, Lieutenant," interrupted Brody. "The seep here is about gone and of little use. We are from Fuerte Viejo and plan to arrive back there by noon."

The lieutenant nodded to his corporal, who ordered a dismount. "Sir, I have no quarrel with civilians in this area. Your business is just that: your business. It is not my concern as long as it does not interfere with my orders or official US government or military affairs. But the good chief here indicates that you have one single Apache in your party. He will be arrested and taken off your hands."

CHAPTER 60

FRIDAY MORNING

From his hiding place, Walking Knife could see nothing but grass and dust. This Felipe had placed him behind the boulder and covered him with what loose soil and stones were available, not that it amounted to much of anything more than the barest concealment. Still, in light of the question of the killings at the Place of Two Strange Men, he was grateful for Felipe's actions. It was indicative of the conundrum that faced Apaches. Even those who lived down in Mexico held its citizens in disgust and disdain, yet for generations, for as long as anyone alive could remember, the People had stolen Mexican youths and adopted them as their own, augmenting their own meager numbers and replacing those who had in turn been abducted by the Mexicans. By living with the band of Cochise as a boy, Felipe had become human, whereas if he had not been adopted, Walking Knife could kill him now as he would a horse, anywhere, without compunction. No doubt if Felipe had not had the experience, he would be ready to kill him too.

He could not hear any of the conversations below him. That meant everything must be going well. The white leader, the enforcer of rules, was successfully deferring the soldiers. There was no danger. Or did that mean that they were approaching him stealthily? He closed his eyes to focus on what he heard, to limit the stimuli that was coming to him and possibly distracting him. He tried to concentrate. There was nothing to hear but his own heart-beat. Finally, after what seemed a long period of time, he heard horses whinny, but no voices accompanied them. Time lapsed and he continued to concentrate, fighting the urge to shift his position or move over the top of the hill. Hearing the crunch of the dry ground, he attempted to flatten himself even more and move ever so incrementally into the shadow of the large stone. *Perhaps Ussen lives, and perhaps I should have kept his songs.*

CHAPTER 61
FRIDAY MORNING

The heat in O'Meara's small office was stifling. The water crock had not been refreshed this morning, and the stale contents from last night would soon evaporate. At one time he had regretted not having his office in the front of the Nantucket Whaler, where he could have viewed his domain, his kingdom, and watched it grow. Now, at this moment, he was glad he faced the fields and distant mountains on the western horizon. The town, his town, was going to dry up and disintegrate into the same worthless rubble as he had found. With no vein of ore discovered, with the deaths of the McCord brothers (or husband and wife), and with the constant threat from Apaches and Los Hombres, the whites would soon abandon their lots and claims and head for California or Colorado. Even now a wagon of three miners was leaving, and he could hear the small crowd in the street calling to them, though the words were indistinct. Others would be going soon.

The Mexicans and Papagos would stay, of course, but only because they had no place to go. They offered him nothing in the way of wealth or fortune, not even in five or ten years down the road. They had been here for hundreds of years and might be here for a hundred more, but they would exist without him. He too had decided it was time to retreat and regroup.

He took a pewter cup and dipped it into the crock to withdraw tepid water. Should he make Micah aware that he planned to leave? He thought he must. Whereas he himself had made very little money from Fuerte Viejo, he was sure that Micah had come out deep in the red. The Yankee shopkeeper was a bastard, but he was family, and therefore O'Meara felt he owed his cousin something in the way of an explanation and escape.

And what of Bendix? That despicable cur, that fat bug of a man, had proven that he was dishonest. But he knew too much—the wagon delivery, the hiring of Greybib, the sending of bottled messages in the middle of the desert. It was too dangerous to abandon him at this point. O'Meara needed to get him to some other destination and then cut him loose. But where to go from here?

He slammed the pewter cup into the crock. "Damn! Damn it all!"

CHAPTER 62

FRIDAY MORNING

The lieutenant, troopers, and the two scouts dismounted and took positions about fifty feet from the posse, forming a distinct camp of their own. They arranged themselves in a large circle and went through the normal preparation of camp, throwing down accoutrements and stretching stiff limbs.

"Foster, picket our horses away from the others. If we're subject to a surprise raid, we don't want the added injury of losing them."

Without reply, a faceless trooper collected reins and led the army horses some distance away. To anyone who had lived on the frontier, or in any rural setting, it was a safe and acknowledged practice. Horses, being simultaneously followers, prey-minded, and stupid, were given to group movement and panic. If a snake or Apache raider or any danger in general attempted to "shoo" a horse, the others would follow suit. By separating the troopers' mounts from those of the posse, one group of the other would be able to keep their horses with them and remain mobile should an incident arise.

The lieutenant approached the posse with his white scout following and the black scout even farther behind him. "Who is in charge here?"

"I guess you could say I am. I'm Edwin Brody from Fuerte Viejo."

While the white scout's eyes widened in recognition of the name, the lieutenant seemed ignorant or oblivious. "We have been traveling through the night. A band of hostiles struck across the border and close to Fort Crittenden. Early on they left a broad trail, herding a small number of cattle." He paused to arch and stretch his back. "But they broke into smaller groups until we lost them all in darkness. Shame. We think there is a captive Mexican woman with them.

"Anyway, Mr. Brody," he continued. "I hope you will accept us as campmates. We would like to rest for a short period and refresh ourselves at the spring. Further, we would like to see that Apache. We know he is here."

"Like I said, we are leaving, so you're welcome to it," replied Brody, motioning to the seep behind him. "Water is about gone, I think. It's scarcer now than before, or so Felipe says." He nodded to his young companion.

"This is Felipe, our right hand and guide. This is Professor Metz and McLeroy Banks, and that man carrying the little howitzer up on the hill is Spencer." He paused, realizing that while Spence had come down as directed, he had then gone up the hill again as Felipe had come down. He immediately questioned whether that was to cover the Indian or to take an advantageous position in the event of a violent altercation. "And as for the Indian, well, he was here as late as this morning."

The white scout, finally seeing an opening to speak, tried to approach Brody. "Say, are you the same Edwin Brody from El Paso? I was there when—"

"Let it go," warned Brody, continuing to stare the man down long after the words were finished.

Again the lieutenant was oblivious to the tension, but Banks and the professor exchanged glances. Felipe looked back at them to see if they had caught the white scout's question. The officer squatted on his haunches. "If it is not too personal, are you men...?"

Krieg stopped, catching himself being too inquisitive. "Beg your pardon, but you men are surely brave. Here I am, hesitant to take the field with twelve troopers, while you seem confident in your small number. Would you like to ride in our company or join us? Your expertise and our combined firepower could prove to be of mutual benefit."

"I think it best that we get to the point here, Lieutenant," Brody countered. "You said you know the Apache is here. Perhaps you meant that you knew he *was* here, or had been here. There was an Apache here last night, but he isn't in camp now. You don't see him and neither do I."

"I did not expect to find him," said the officer with a smile. "The chief was pretty much distraught and out of sorts. His son translated and led us to believe that there is a renegade among you. That seemed unlikely, but we thought it best to investigate. I would be correct in saying that the Indian was here, is that right? These Papagos were not leading us astray, I bet. Sir, if you tell me that the Apache is no longer in your custody, or that he has traveled on, then I will not press you further."

"Well, you would be absolutely right, sir, absolutely right about Chief Juan. But—" He indicated the blanket again. "We asked him about water and roaming bands. He sat on that red blanket there and we asked him. There was no further discussion. He was traveling alone."

"He came from the north, I think," volunteered Felipe. "He said that he had been with some Arivaipa and that those people had gone to Santa Ynez. He was a Red Paint Apache who came from far to the east, in what is New Mexico. Those are the people of Mangas Colorado and Vitorio."

Brody picked up again. "Felipe lived among the Apaches for some while, and from him I know that the hostiles have very strong kinship ties. Although he told us he was going east, I do not think it unreasonable to assume that he went south to Cochise's band.

Eastward could have been a lie. You know, in case..." He let the words trail off.

The black scout nodded as the officer, Brody, and Felipe pondered the situation and the white scout made his way to the seep of refreshing water. As he slung his canteen into the slow-moving trickle, he was approached by Banks and the professor.

CHAPTER 63

FRIDAY MORNING

With no pretense of casual behavior, Banks and Metz rushed to the grizzled white scout. Good manners called for introductions and a slow approach to the question at hand, but they were too intrigued. Banks went right at the stranger, rushing him as if he held the knowledge of a secret treasure or mystical art.

"You knew Brody in El Paso? Did you say that?"

"No, I said I was there when it happened. People don't listen."

"Well, begging your pardon, but what happened? We think very highly of Edwin, but you have a story on you. We'd like to know it."

The wrinkled face smirked with the acknowledgement of importance. "It was late last summer. I was in El Paso in between scouts." He continued to fill and empty the canteen to clean it as best he could. "You know I am quite in demand in Texas. I've campaigned against Comanches, Kiowas, and, during the war, Cheyenne and Arapahos. That was in Kansas, of course."

Banks stifled the urge to both roll his eyes and tell the man to get to the damned point. "You're a very knowledgeable frontiersman, that is for sure. What happened in El Paso?"

"Well, like I said," continued the scout, with obvious irritation at having been interrupted, "it was late summer, but not as hot there as it is here. It's not much of a town, and there isn't much to do but farm cotton, trade with the greasers, or get drunk. I was going to work my way up the Rio Grande or Rio Bravo, and I was in town just for a night. There was this little saloon called the Customs House. It wasn't but a fifteen-by-fifteen adobe with two wooden tables and a plank bar. But anyhow, that man over there was sitting at a table, minding his own business. I was standing at the bar when these three men came in, and you could tell they were looking for a bad time. You've seen men like that, just itching for a scrap."

"Yeah, go on."

"Well, they didn't say 'hello' or 'go to hell' to me. Guess they could see that I would not stand for it. Or maybe they knew who I was."

Or maybe they just figured you were a nothing little insignificant shit of a bug, thought Banks, but he kept that to himself.

"But after a few drinks, they decided they were tired of standing and wanted a table, your friend's table. So the biggest one proceeded to kick the chair and say real mean, 'Kinda selfish to take a table for just yourself.' And your friend over there says back, 'I don't know if you are asking or telling, but I own this table for the night.'"

"He is a hard man for certain. I would think he would be well prepared for a scrap," interjected the professor.

"Hard man? Hardest I ever saw. Why, when that big man pulled Brody up to get him out of that seat, your friend just pulled a big Remington and stuck it right in the man's belly. He pulled the trigger, and even though it was muffled, it was loud. That big man let out a howl, and one of his partners did too. That big ball went through the first man, clean through, and hit the second in the stomach too. Two men with one shot. That was just luck and trajectory, but it acted like a slap in the face to that third man, who burst out the side door like horses was pulling him. That little room was packed, but it emptied out like an anthill. I stayed just 'cause I was trapped by all the others. Those two sons of bitches rolled on the floor and howled and carried on so."

"Anything happen after that?" asked Banks.

"Yeah, he sat back down and kept drinking. I cannot say it was like nothing happened, because that fellow looked like he was going to cry. He even shook a little. But he sat there and did not move one inch to get away until a lawman came. The big man died pretty quickly. We explained what happened, and he was allowed to remain out while a quick coroner's jury determined that the big man had died of a bad temperament caused by a buildup of bile. Pretty funny, that. The wounded one was put up in the hotel, but I don't know what became of him. I left town the next morning."

"That is certainly the kind of harrowing tale one would expect from the frontier—men without law and without the moral restraint that society normally imposes," the professor mused. The scout's response was to eye him up and down as one would a museum curiosity, then continue with his canteen's ablutions.

Banks started to respond and then caught himself. "Well, thank you for your time, sir. Like I said, we think a great deal of Mr. Brody. Like you," he said, attempting flattery. "He is a man of considerable talent and knowledge. We are certainly obliged to hear more of him." He quickly pulled the professor back to the confines of their own camp equipment and, he hoped, out of earshot of anyone else.

"Professor, I am not a man of science like yourself. Are you familiar with melancholia?"

"I must confess that I am not. Thought I attempt to be a well-rounded scholar, I am not one for the sciences of the mind. Of course..."

"Professor, I have no schooling and am not academically inclined. However, I am a student of men, of people and their character. This lawman is very forthright and honest. I believe he is also very dangerous. Here and there, among men and women, I have seen melancholia and what it does. This lawman is on a binge, not of alcohol but of sadness and despondency. If he has an episode here with just us, I fear it may be ugly. To put it to a point, Professor, I believe we are in great danger."

CHAPTER 64

FRIDAY MORNING

After shaking hands, the lieutenant returned to his men. The black scout hesitated, and then, as an afterthought, turned to the seep to fill his canteen. He was stopped by a restraining hand from Brody.

"You appear to have an active mind but a quiet mouth. Let's fill your canteen together."

"My daddy says the wisest man does the littlest talking. I sure don't plan to talk across nobody nohow."

"If you have something to say, this would be the time and place for it. If you fear retribution, I can assure you that Arizona welcomes all. There is none of the effrontery you might find as a Negro in the east. We have among us whites, blacks, Catholics, Mormons…"

The scout paused and stared straight ahead, clearly pondering what he had heard and what he wanted to say. "I hear you saying I can speak my mind? I can speak my conscience?"

"Yep, if you can give an honest opinion and not be rude."

There was a humorless laugh from the black man and he repeated the phrase to himself. "Not be rude." He continued to stare straight ahead with something close to anger in his eyes. "No, sir, it ain't rudeness. It is the truth I want to say."

"Then say it. I do not intend to stand in the hot sun while you contemplate your words. Be plain!"

"All right, all right, I will do just that. Now that scout there—O'Connor is his name." The anger was now evident in his speech. "That man may know all about fighting some Indians. He knows all about Comanche and Kiowas and whatnot. But he don't know a thing, not one damned thing, about fighting Apaches. He is going to get every one of us killed."

"How so?"

"All the time talking about them counting coups and riding ponies. He say they all going to ride around us in a circle in the open where we can see 'em real plain. He told the lieutenant there that he's been in a wickiup and seen scalps. But these Indians don't be where you can see 'em, and they don't take no scalps. If he's wrong about all that, then what else is he wrong about?"

Perplexed, Brody turned to Felipe, who nodded. "Felipe, that sure sounds like one lie on top of another. Apaches sure don't ride where you can see them, and they don't take scalps, do they?"

"No, Mister Edwin. They..." He paused to find the right words. "They cut off a scalp, maybe, but they do not keep it. It would bring sickness with it. They cut off parts of the body, but they keep nothing. Those things are dirty."

The black scout began again. "I can't tell if he is leading us to Apaches to fight them, or if he is trying not to find them so we don't. I know what I would do, but I ain't been asked."

Brody turned again to the scout. "And you don't think the army will listen to you? Because you're colored?"

"You know what's gonna happen to me if I cross talk that O'Connor and call him a fool in front of that Yankee cavalryman? Besides, who is gonna to listen to a Negro way out here in the middle of nowhere?"

"I'm thinking everyone should. You know your business. I told you, Arizona is wide open. Let's go talk to the lieutenant. No, better yet, you stay here and I'll go talk to him. You just get your water and relax. I'll get that yellow leg straightened out. And just how in the hell did you get way out here, anyway? Nobody is from here, so where are you from?"

"I come from the piney woods of Louisiana. I been here with my daddy for a bit. We come from Houston to San Antonio to Mesilla. My daddy lives in Santa Ynez, but I ain't seen him for a year or more. I took a freighting job and then another one and then another one, all up and down the Rio Bravo. You know it as the Rio Grande. But I took a scout job just to come home again."

"Wait, how is your dad called?"

"Old Abraham. Well, that would be what he calls himself. His name is Abraham, but Old fits him 'cause he was old when I was borned, and I reckon he was old when he was borned too. He was borned hobblin' around, but he is a hard worker. I am proud of him, and we gonna see each other again once this scout is through."

Brody broke into a grin. "Do you mean to tell me your daddy is Old Abraham? Is he about blind but a good man nonetheless? Well, let me and Felipe have a word with this yellow leg, and you just go and sit a spell. He will listen to us or else." He paused as he gave more consideration to a thought. "Unless you'd rather abandon this scout and come with us. You're less than a day's ride from Fuerte Viejo right now, and that is where your daddy is."

"No, sir, but thank you just the same. My word is good, and if I say I'm a scout, then I am bound to finish the job. If the lieutenant will listen to me, we will head south and look for sign. We been crossin' the trail of soldiers for three days. I think they is more soldiers out than Apaches right now. But if he wants to find them, I will get it done. You just please tell my daddy I will see him by and by real soon."

Together, Brody and Felipe pulled Lieutenant Krieg aside and gave him a moment's worth of education. Almost unnoticed, Pedro left his father and dismounted his pinto, hitching it on the picket line with the Anglos' horses.

CHAPTER 65

FRIDAY NOON

El Gato and Los Hombres fanned out across the road leading into Fuerte Viejo. It was noon, and the glint of the blistering sun on the brass rifles forced them to squint to an even greater degree than they would have under normal circumstances. But they did not worry about the reflections being seen by the poor inhabitants ahead, for the denizens of the little village had no means of defense anyway. The Anglos would be drunk and unaware, the Mexican farmers asleep in their hammocks and pallets. It would be fun.

"Remember, my friends. Do not think about women and children. If you want to shoot, just shoot. If one or two die, the others will not be so quick to fight back. Do not bother with the fucking church. It is the whites who have the money, and that big bastard—the one who owns the town—he has everything and we will get it from him. Do you understand?"

"We know, boss, we know," answered Gordito. "And that lawman fucker, what of him?" He grinned with enthusiasm, each white tooth fringed with black decay. "We will bleed him and teach him about Los Hombres, yes?"

El Gato looked at him with no hint of mercy or compassion. "That fucker will wish he was dead long before death comes to him. He will scream like Jesus on the cross." He changed his tone to a high-pitched feminine whine. "'Why have you forsaken my poor soul?'" And he gave a wicked laugh.

Los Hombres, even Gordito, felt a pang of conscience and fear. Where they had been brave a moment before, they now trembled and their stomachs felt like stone. This day, now that El Gato had committed blasphemy, would be a very bad day to die. They were sinners and had no qualms about their actions and their eventual fate, but no sane man tempted God, and no sane man mocked Jesus. This was a curse upon the whole undertaking.

Their leader gave Midnight Sky a hard kick and started to town. The rest held their horses firm, and it was several seconds before they followed. Vengeful God or no, nobody disobeyed El Gato. God's wrath was later, while El Gato's wrath meant death today. They collectively hoped that if death did come, it would be without eternal damnation.

CHAPTER 66

FRIDAY AFTERNOON

He was covered in dirt and grass and he had picked up some brambles in his shoes, which caused him great pain. However, trained as a warrior, Walking Knife continued running and succeeded in putting the pain out of his mind. While the white soldiers and the friends of the Mexican, Felipe, had been talking, he had stolen away. Another white man, one with a very nice short rifle and a fresh wound on his head, had abetted his escape.

With tension at its greatest, and with Walking Knife running out of soil with which to cover himself, the white man had given him a signal. He had prodded him with the butt of that rifle and tapped the barrel, saying, "Boom. Boom. *Cuando fuego usted va este, comprende?*" He then pointed toward the east.

It was the Mexican tongue. The white man was telling him that he was going to shoot, but obviously not at him. Was it to be a distraction, or was he going to shoot at the soldiers? Just four seasons ago, the whites had conducted a big fight with each other, but that was supposed to be finished. He pointed to the man and asked, "*Usted* boom, *yo?*" He pointed to himself and then to the eastern horizon.

"*Sí, sí.*" The white man held up his hand to show that it would be a moment. Then the man walked far down the ridge in a southern direction. When he had traveled far enough to be as tall as Walking Knife's thumbnail, he pointed at the ground and fired. Then he took the fine small rifle and thrust the butt at the ground repeatedly. He shouted white man's words. Walking Knife did not know their meaning, but he could guess that they meant "snake." Walking Knife gathered on his haunches and sprinted over the grassy ridge, knowing that if the soldiers and those nasty Papagos were truly distracted, he could go straight toward home.

Ahead of him and only four days away were the villages of the Red Paint People. He would return to the place of his birth and roll in the four directions in order to celebrate his safe return. He would stay in the cool mountains and refresh himself where the springs were cool and never ran dry. And he would return to the teachings of his childhood and the ways of Ussen.

CHAPTER 67

FRIDAY AFTERNOON

Verly Harvill sat in her favorite chair, which allowed her to look at the wide street and also gave a good view of the open desert beyond. Frequently she studied the outlined summits of the gray peaks on the horizon, and she had done so often enough to where she could identify them, if only by the names she had created. She had given each a title, and she wondered if they ever saw snow or if they were no more than jagged upthrusts and sunbaked rocks that gave purchase to nothing but cactus and thorn. Probably just the latter, she thought. If anything was cool in Arizona, it was too far away to be seen from Fuerte Viejo.

From the middle of town, there were shouts punctuated with gunfire, a lot of gunfire. Either Apaches had struck the village or some miner had come in with news of a good ore sample and was hurrahing the town. She put down her piece of lace and walked to the glass door to peer down into the main part of town. Suddenly she jumped in horror as two fiendish men in sombreros peered in through the glass. They had seemingly come from nowhere. Despite her being obviously rattled, they showed no expression whatsoever, and as one they brought the butts of their rifles down hard through the glass.

Around the corner along Miner's Row, Big Sarah was just stepping out of Hannah Wheeler's house when a large group of men rode through the town, firing as they went. From their sombreros and dress, she determined that this was no celebration; this was an armed attack. With clear judgment overruling her fear, she turned on her heel and pushed through the door that was just being closed.

"Mrs. Wheeler, where is your boy? And if you've got a gun about, you'd better give it to me quick." She sounded as breathless as if she had just run a mile.

Dumbfounded, Mrs. Wheeler stood for several seconds, mouth agape, not comprehending what was going on even as she turned to the sound of gunfire, attempting mindlessly to peer through the walls of the cabin. She turned to Sarah again and gave a shrug of incomprehension.

"Mrs. Wheeler, where is your boy?" Sarah asked again. She closed the door behind her and gave the knob a momentary glance, looking in vain for a lock. There was none. She was making her way to the fireplace for a tool or weapon when Hannah Wheeler grasped the severity of the event.

"Oh, dear Lord, those are the bandits, the Mexicans that we… oh, dear Lord, Johnny." She ran to the door and flung it open. Already Johnny was making his way to the house, and they collided with enough force to send them both backward a step. Quickly, quite aware that their lives depended on it, she flung him inside. And her husband, where was he? At the Nantucket Whaler, Micah's, or maybe that Mexican sin hole, La Cantina? She looked about for a weapon before her eyes finally locked on Sarah. She was holding a poker in one hand and Hannah's very large kitchen knife in the other.

CHAPTER 68

FRIDAY AFTERNOON

While Los Hombres emptied the store of its goods and tried to find suitable women for their lustful ambitions, El Gato, Flaco, DeJesus, and Renaldo stood in O'Meara's office. They were so supremely confident that they felt no need to rush through the confrontation. The old drunk bastard would open his mouth soon enough. He was a coward, so it would not take long, and they could be patient. From outside, rifle and pistol fire gave evidence that they were in complete control of the town, as they had known they would be.

"Do not be greedy, man. You tell El Gato where the money is and you live. We do not wish to fire the bank and, uh, burn the money, no? We burn the bank and the money is lost. Then you lose and I lose. But if you give us the money, then you save bank and you fill it again. Tell El Gato, friend. We find out anyway. Do not make trouble."

"How dare you!" O'Meara said. "I am the big rooster of this town. I have shared with you and you have made a good profit. You know full well that this arrangement has been good to you. I have allowed you to pirate my wagons and even given you those good rifles. You owe me, you insolent bug. You are a boil on my ass, and I will have you for this."

"You talk fast, but I hear ugly things. I do not like when American fuckers say ugly things. No fucker talks to me that way, Mexican or white." Secretly, El Gato cared not what anyone said about him. His power was absolute, and he did not feel insulted or threatened. Only it was necessary to claim otherwise in front of his men. He nodded to Renaldo, who swung his brass Winchester hard into O'Meara's jaw. The big man was too stunned to cry out but held his face with both hands. Two big saucer eyes stared out between crimson-colored hands.

"How dare you?" he mumbled between his fingers.

"Dare! Dare! Dare! What is to dare? I dare this and I dare that, what is the difference?" El Gato laughed. He took enormous glee both in besting O'Meara and in frustrating him to the point of tears. To destroy anything, man or beast, was pleasurable. "We do what we do. Hurry, old friend. We do not want the fire to get the bank. Tell us the number to the *caja* and where all your money is. Is money worth to die for?"

O'Meara began to cry, not in pain but in helpless frustration. Everything had gone to ruin for him. He had tried so hard, yet now everything he had earned, everything he was entitled to, was slipping from his fingers. His body shook as he gave silent, gasping sobs.

Downstairs, under the bar, Bendix huddled, hoping that no Hombre would venture behind the counter.

CHAPTER 69

FRIDAY AFTERNOON

From several miles away, they could see black smoke rising from the area of Fuerte Viejo. It was dense and black, the smoke of something menacing and dangerous, not the innocent purple of a brush fire or the white from a campsite. They kicked their horses to a gallop. Closer to the town, the boom of rifles and pop of pistols could be heard. Tiny black figures, like ants in the distance, moved back and forth across the wide street.

"More Apaches?" inquired Professor Metz and another Anglo whose voice Brody could not identify among the murmurs and stomping horses.

Before he could answer, or because the question had not been directed to any one person, Felipe responded excitedly, "No. *Son Hombres!* Los Hombres!"

"Listen up," hollered Brody, being unusually authoritative. The group reined their horses just before the southernmost field, having broken off from the road in order to take a more direct path. He began again but caught himself. "Wait, was anyone here an officer?"

Banks and Spencer shook their heads and Heydt responded, "Just a corporal, Edwin."

"Then we do it my way." He spurred his mount to face the group, and the horse danced in anxious anticipation. "We ride in as a group, hard and fast. If anyone gets too far ahead, pull up. We won't go in strung out over a distance but all together. Head for La Cantina, *now!*"

The horses, their excitement contagious, plunged forward. All the riders, save Spence, drew their revolvers. Even Metz had a small hand pistol displayed, waving it aloft while leaning well forward and spurring hard. There was no need for anyone to express concern, for they all felt it. It was concern for their loved ones and for the familiar yet nameless faces, white and brown, and it was every bit as infectious as the excitement among their horses. The thundering hooves drowned out the sound of the gunfire from town, but there was still enough powder smoke to indicate that Fuerte Viejo was occupied by a hostile group. The plume of black smoke still poured forth from what they could now see was the warehouse beside the bank.

The horsemen split to either side of La Cantina, but Pedro and Felipe continued in through the gaping back door and rode into the building itself. There was a crashing of tables and chairs and two very loud shots. As Brody, Heydt, Banks, Metz, and Spencer dismounted under the ramada, two more shots sounded from inside La Cantina, and two Mexican gunmen staggered out front. One grasped his stomach with both hands and grimaced in pain before falling to his knees and then finally his face. The other, in red shirt and red pants, looked about in bewilderment, his shock as absolute as his companion's agony. He apparently died as he stood, because he made no effort to throw out his arms to buffer his fall to the sandy floor.

Scanning in all directions at once, Brody saw that though the Mexican renegades were everywhere, they seemed to be congregated in three places, all in the Anglo portion of Fuerte Viejo. A small number milled about at Micah's, a few more positioned themselves at the Nantucket Whaler, and others were at the burning warehouse building and the bank next to it. Some stragglers rode up and down the street on fast horses, shooting glass and splintering wood. All carried new brass Winchesters.

None of the resident miners were shooting at the outlaws, and those visible seemed to be standing in awe at what they were seeing. Some few appeared as dead bodies in the street. If not dead, they were so wounded as not to move. Likewise, none of the returning posse fired but held themselves in check, seemingly waiting for Brody's instructions. Suddenly, as he pointed to Micah's, a large shadow enveloped them, blotting out the sun above. Like scattered hens Brody and the others flew in all directions, firing pistols upward as they scrambled. Bits of splintered wood preceded the fall of a large Mexican who collapsed through the ramada. As he fell in a heap on an old mission-style table, Brody approached him to take a second look. The Hombre wore a soft blue shirt with a blue paisley pattern. It had been stolen from a clothesline some months before. It had been his only other shirt.

Pedro and Felipe emerged from the darkness of La Cantina clutching shiny Winchester repeating rifles. "They are full of bullets, very heavy," said Pedro.

Felipe looked grim but determined. "We are with you, Mister Edwin."

"Good," answered Brody flatly, his voice exhibiting no more emotion than if he were talking of a horse or giving directions to another town. His face, however, gave evidence of fear or hatred or tension, with his lips pulled back to expose his teeth in a nasty grimace. As he spoke, Banks bent over and took the third Winchester from the Hombre in blue paisley and began loading it from the dead man's belt. Banks moved quickly but with determination, showing great economy of movement.

The lawman issued his plan. "Spence, I want you on the roof and to lay fire onto that bunch at Micah's. We will drive them north and not leave any behind us. Felipe, you and Pedro do the same. Hit Micah's store hard. Make those sons of bitches howl, and clean up that flank. Banks and Heydt, let's go to Nantucket." To himself he added, "And on to Verly's. Please let her be safe."

Leaving Professor Metz to examine the bandits, he turned on his heel and walked calmly up the street as if he were going to get a drink, making his way without crouching or evading the random bullets that flew about. Banks and Heydt looked at one another incredulously before they both fell in behind. Banks followed Brody, trying to see around the corner to Miner's Row and to where Big Sarah lived. He wanted to see that she was safe, but to go now, to cross the street before they had wrested control from the bandits, would do no one any good.

As they made their way from La Cantina, a drunken Hombre rode past the trio in a blaze, then reined in his horse as he glanced back to make sure of what he had just seen. Brody raised his pistol but Banks was faster. He put a round from his new rifle into the man's shoulder. The outlaw landed awkwardly on his head and did not move. Behind them, what sounded like a company of infantry opened up from their starting point.

The big-bore Spencer boomed twice, and then Pedro and Felipe opened up on the men across the street at Micah's. As dust, wood, brick, and glass erupted in tiny bits, the Mexicans variously staggered, froze in bewilderment, or bumped into each other in what would have been comedic in other circumstances. The collective movement seemed to increase the size of the meager group, but it was a rapidly dissolving illusion. As Spencer emptied his Spencer carbine, the last Hombre limped behind the store or perhaps even farther. Two lay on Micah's veranda, and two others had tumbled into the street. If they were not dead, they were too incapacitated to cause further harm.

Pedro smiled broadly and spoke in a mumbled tone to the dead men who rested almost two hundred feet away. "Say *no más, no más.*"

Spencer shouted at his companions as if they were not right next to him. "See if those dead men have any more bullets on them. Then we will go to Micah's and work from that side. We're going to hit them again." To himself he added, "God, this feels good."

CHAPTER 70

FRIDAY AFTERNOON

Through the front window, Big Sarah and Hannah Wheeler could see the corpulent bandit making his way up Miner's Row. He was dressed much more plainly than the others they could see, plain brown shirt and plain white paints with silver coins as conchos, but he was well fed and looked like he might be powerful as well. He was checking the doors of each dwelling and entering briefly, obviously finding nothing of interest. As he made his way to Hannah Wheeler's place, Big Sarah moved to the wall beside the door. After taking a deep breath, she gave an approving nod. As the knob jiggled, Hannah flung the door open and took quick steps back, either to avoid danger or to lure the big man in, even she herself was not sure which. She held the knife before her, but she looked weak and would not have menaced anyone.

"Ah, *bonita*, you look very good to me. We will be friends quick." Gordito lumbered through the doorway, blotting out the mission ruins behind him. He hesitated as he caught sight of Johnny, who was making a feeble attempt to merge himself with the back wall. "My amigo, my friend. We have a good time too, eh?"

There was a sound that was as soft as the punching of a pillow yet hard like the striking of wood as Sarah planted the poker into the back of the bandit's skull. His eyes widened as he leaned well forward in an involuntary effort to steady himself. There was a moment of stunned inactivity by all before both women screamed and jumped as an unexpected gunshot roared in the tiny confines of the cabin. The big man fell backward and his face disappeared in a mask of crimson pouring from a hole in his forehead. They both turned to see Johnny holding his dad's navy revolver. They jumped again as he fired a second and third time.

CHAPTER 71

FRIDAY AFTERNOON

The bandits loitering in front of the Nantucket Whaler had just taken notice of Brody, Banks, and Heydt when El Gato and the others shoved a bleeding Farrell O'Meara out onto the veranda. His mouth was red from blood, and his clothes were disheveled from far more than a staggering drunken binge. One of the Hombres pointed to the three Anglos and the crowd of bandits on the veranda, including the newcomers and O'Meara, and all turned to face them. O'Meara was the first to speak.

"For God's sake, do something, Edwin. This was not supposed happen. They were never supposed to enter the town. It's all gone wrong."

Brody shook his head, not understanding the meaning, but not giving up on the notion that these men needed to be killed. His pistol was still aimed in their direction but at no one person in particular. "What? What do you mean?"

"Ho, ho. This is the sheriff man?" laughed the one who seemed to be in charge. This man then turned to O'Meara. "You did not tell this one of our arrangement? You no tell him we partners? Now this fucker is *celoso*. He want some of the money too, I bet." He laughed again and shouted *"Dispararle!"* In an instant the men raised their rifles, but it was too late. Brody's pistol shot flames three times in quick succession, and more flame erupted past his ear as Heydt and Banks shot into the mass. Several men fell to their knees and more fell on their backs. Those that were unhurt or showed no visible wounds ran across the wide street to the bank. Two more fell in the street as the lawman drew his other pistol and opened up.

"My God, there are dead men everywhere," said Hedyt, uncharacteristically crude. He fumbled with the lever action of the rifle, perturbed by the sudden endeavor he had been called to perform. Fear and excitement were robbing him of his motor skills. "Good Lord, I never thought I would have to do something like this again. My hands are shaking." He finally collapsed into a sitting position in the street. "Oh, I am done for."

"You are not hit. Good God, man, get to cover," said Brody, but it was Banks who reached down and pulled him to a standing position.

They raced onto the veranda where O'Meara knelt and clasped his hands about the railing. A red hole in his thigh pulsated with flowing blood. Apparently one of his rescuers had shot him by accident, or perhaps the bullet had carried through the body of one of Los Hombres. To his credit, or through the effects of shock, he did not cry out.

"That one, Edwin." He threw his head in the direction of the street. "That one crawling, he is their leader. That is El Gato. Kill him quickly before he makes his escape. We mustn't allow him to get away. He'll talk."

"He will keep," replied Brody. He was finally squatting in what Banks and Heydt considered a moment of lucidity. Maybe, they thought, he'd finally succumbed to the good sense to hide and make his body smaller. It was if he had just now become cognizant of the danger. Both pistols were on the wooden boardwalk beside him. "I have two pistols half loaded. Why did I do such a thing? It seems my wits have left me."

No, thought Heydt. *You finally woke up from that stupor. Now let us keep each other alive.*

As the constable spilled loose bullets and attempted to reload the twin Navies, a cacophony of gunfire issued from across the street. Pedro, Felipe, and Spence were on Micah's elevated veranda, pouring a devastating fire onto the bank and those around it. An occasional cloud of red erupted as bullets found soft tissue or shattered skulls. More of Los Hombres fell, and as a group they gave the appearance of defeat. Those upright recognized the danger and futility of fighting the townsmen from both the saloon and the general store. Los Hombres that could mounted random horses and scurried down their only venue of escape, Miner's Row and the purple hills beyond. Those they left behind lay still or writhed in agony, a testament to the talent and vindictiveness of Brody and his men.

"I must see to Verly," Brody said. "Don't give chase to those. There is no need. They have taken their licking and will not reorganize or regroup for some time."

"Wait, Edwin," Banks said. "There may be more about, and we can get some of these farmers and miners armed and with us. We don't have an idea what is down at the homes. Heydt and I still need you."

"See to arming the men, then. Grab these son-of-a-bitch miners just standing around. I must see to Verly and her well-being. I will go to see Marianna and Sarah directly. Do what you feel or what you must."

With both pistols in hand and fully loaded, he made his way up the street. He became aware of the warehouse next to the bank, enveloped in flame, the dry wood hissing and cracking. Certainly he had noticed it already; its smoke had served as the beacon bringing them into town at a gallop. Yet it had been a feature of the background, no part of it interfering with his thought processes. The roar of the flames had surely been audible, but only now did he become mindful of it, truly see it and accept it. As tense as the situation, as anxious as he had been in most all his conscious moments, he was as calm and clear as a man could be. And he was aware of it. *This is my gift,* he thought. *This is what I can do that others cannot: dispatch evil with impunity, blocking out all else from my mind. I may hurt tonight or tomorrow, and I may fear that I lost control. But the fear that checks others and keeps them from acting is not in me. The distractions that keep others from focusing are unknown to me. This is my gift.*

As if in answer, two men emerged from Verly Harvill's door, sombreros thrown well back on their heads. They gave a quick glance at Brody and then down the street and southward to see many of their confederates crumpled in heaps here and there. Without raising their rifles to provide covering fire, they mounted up and road northward on the road to the Pima Villages so far away.

"Oh, my God! Verly!" Brody ran the remaining distance and burst through the door without hesitation. All was dark, and it was a moment before his eyes adjusted. He looked about at eye level before movement from below attracted his attention. Verly lay on the floor, her torn white dress pulled over her like a sheet to provide some shred of modesty. Tears were streaming down her cheeks, washing away her lavish paint in rivulets. "Please go away, Edwin. You cannot see me like this."

"Verly, what have they done? What have they done?"

"Edwin get out!" she screamed. "You cannot see this. Let me be, damn it all."

He stepped back in confusion and frustration but caught himself before exiting. "No, not before you tell me what I can do." He squatted instinctually to lessen the imposing position of his body in relation to her, fumbling awkwardly to reach out. "Let me get you a dress. Or may I get Sarah? Please tell me how to help."

She began to bawl, great racking sobs that shook her. "Damn you, just leave!" she screamed even more emphatically than before. "Just go away and leave me be. Please. You don't want to see me."

"No, Miss Verly. You are mine." He crept closer and pulled her tightly to him, hugging her fiercely and allowing her to hug him back in pitiful, helpless frustration. "Just cry out. Just cry out and let me take care of you. Let's get you to bed and I will send for Big Sarah. And when I get back..." He pulled back to look her in the eyes. "When I get back, I will never leave you again, I promise."

CHAPTER 72

FRIDAY AFTERNOON

El Gato hurt all over. He did not know where the bullets had entered, nor how they had traveled and coursed through his body, ravaging tissue and bone. Perhaps he was physically able to move, but he hurt too much to try. To raise himself on one elbow was not so bad, but crawling was not even a consideration. Looking about, he could see that a tall blond man was directing some of the townspeople into a bucket brigade. Some of the bastard farmers were even now, in the heat of battle, stripping his men of boots and gear. Then he realized it: the battle was over. There was no more shooting, only the hiss and roar of the old wooden building and the shouts of a few people here and there. All his men and all those shiny new Winchesters were gone. Were they all dead, or had the survivors ridden away and forsaken him? Was he not to be rescued? Would he live long enough to have a rope stretch his neck? The dread was almost enough to block out his present pain. Then he remembered his earlier words. He remembered that he had mocked the Son. Ice ran through his veins to replace the fire of pain.

From up the street he saw the sheriff man coming. This man walked with determination and anger. "You win today, gringo," El Gato said. "Put a hat over my face. The sun hurt my eyes."

The angry man's only answer was to draw both pistols from his waist. But once they were out and pointed at him, the man returned one to its holster. His one free hand grabbed El Gato by the hair and pulled his back up in a painful arch.

El Gato screamed in pain. "Son of bitch, you hurt me! Let me go, you bastard. I do not want to die, goddamn you!" But El Gato realized that he would not suffer the lingering death from the hangman.

CHAPTER 73

FRIDAY AFTERNOON

Edwin Brody exited and saw that although there were several dozen miners and farmers on the boardwalks and streets (and Heydt was organizing some of them into a bucket brigade), the Hombres that had fallen remained in place. Those that were dead had been stripped of boots and hats and any other accoutrements that had been determined to be valuable. The unlucky wounded howled in pain as they were forcibly twisted about to be relieved of their goods as well.

Where Miner's Row intersected the street and made a wide expanse in front of the bank, he saw El Gato, who lay still but very much alive. He struggled with his nonresponsive body and gave an arrogant smile.

"You win today, gringo. Put a hat over my face. The sun hurt my eyes."

In answer, Edwin drew both pistols, but then realized he needed a free hand. He knelt and grabbed the outlaw by the hair and placed one of the revolvers in the bandit's mouth. He paused, imagining the back of the man's head exploding into the dust. He stared into the eyes of the killer and watched the man cower even through his own hurt. The man was saying something but the words sounded far off, like they came from a hundred feet away. No, this would not give him any satisfaction, but it would make some way toward punishing them all for Verly's pain. For now, that was all he could offer her.

CHAPTER 74

FRIDAY AFTERNOON

"Edwin, look here." Big Sarah was clutching the Wheeler boy and Banks was on the other side, providing protective support for the youngster. Both Sarah and the boy had tear-tracked faces and had not yet settled themselves. although she seemed to be in better control. Johnny was more dazed than distraught.

"Mr. Constable. Johnny here was the bravest man I have ever seen. Why, he saved his mother and me, sure as the world. Bravest man I ever saw, hands down." She smiled, but it was empty encouragement meant to soothe Johnny's emotions. He was oblivious. Edwin had seen it in the war. The boy's wide, vacant eyes told him that any consoling would need to be done at a later time, when the boy was somewhat aware. For now the boy—or perhaps young man after today—needed a chore or a duty, something to occupy his mind.

"It's over now, Edwin. We done real good today, but let's keep it that way—a good deed. Don't cheat the hangman by killing this bug. Better that sumbitch—excuse me, Johnny—choke on his tongue for a minute than be dispatched so easy. Please. Johnny here needs to know that there is good. He needs to see you do good, to see you do what is right and moral."

Brody looked down again at El Gato's squinting face. He questioned whether that squint was in anticipation of a final gunshot or the overbearing sun. Had not the man said something about needing a hat? Gingerly he pulled the gun barrel from the man's mouth and stuck it to his ear, catching part of the folded skin. Then he pulled the trigger.

"Sarah, Verly needs you. She is in a bad way. Will you go to her, please? I wish to see Marianna. I want to know that she is okay."

Sarah frowned at Brody's words. "God help us, Edwin. I sure will. My poor friend. Mr. Banks, please take this young man back to his mother." Before taking her leave, she was hugged by McLeroy. For what seemed like an eternity, they clutched each other in an emotional embrace. Brody dropped El Gato's head and gave him a hard kick to the ribs, which made the wounded man scream. The scream was high and almost feminine. His writhing accentuated the bloody ear that flopped loosely from his head.

Banks and Brody walked to the jacal with quick and determined strides, Johnny already forgotten and left standing alone in the street. Banks fished a folded paper from his shirt pocket with one hand, and with a quick jerk, he snapped it to a complete size. He offered it to Brody, but it was not acknowledged, not even with a glance. As they walked, Banks left it in the air between them as if it was something neither wanted.

"Okay, Edwin. Just so you know not to change your mind about that El Gato or Farrell O'Meara. Obviously you're in no mood to read this, but I am working in concert with the federal marshal. Like Sarah said, we have done good today, but we cannot kill these men in cold blood, no matter how deserving. That is what keeps us above them. We can hold them under arrest until I can notify the marshal and a circuit judge rides through. Maybe a posse can take them to Prescott."

Brody stopped and grabbed the letter and read it. Though the missive was brief, his mind was beginning to flutter with the events of the day and the realization of what had occurred. It took him several readings before he could fathom the contents. It was a brief explanation of how the bearer had the full confidence of the US Marshall, and that local law enforcement should assist if practical and able.

"I am truly sorry, Edwin. I knew that you could be trusted, really, but I needed evidence to prove that trust. I could not bring you into my confidence without 100 percent surety that you were square. Please forgive me."

"You are excused. There is no harm and you had to be sure, that is understandable. You said El Gato and Farrell O'Meara. You said them both. They are together?"

Banks grabbed his sleeve. "You got it, Edwin. You heard what that son of a bitch said on the balcony. He said that you were left out of the matter, and now you would be jealous. That El Gato said that they were partners and that you would be offended or jealous at being left out of the bag. And you heard O'Meara say that El Gato had to be killed before he could talk."

As he felt Brody pull away, he tightened his grasp and flung the man to the dirt, landing on top of him. He sat on the lawman's chest to pin him down. "No, sir, we are not going to allow this to go any further. Both those men will sit in that godforsaken hole you call a jail and cook like potatoes until the circuit judge comes through. You hear me? You will not commit a murder. I will not allow a good man to sully himself so.

"I'm going to let you up, but there will be no more today. You will not be allowed to do anything that hurts you or brings discredit upon you. I will not allow it. And Verly needs you, man. Do what is right by Verly. Would not going to prison or evading the law hurt her, when she's been hurt so much already?"

Brody nodded. Anything for Verly. "You have my word, Mr. Banks. I give you my word."

CHAPTER 75

FRIDAY EVENING

As could be imagined, the Sam Houston Saloon, the Nantucket Whaler, and La Cantina were full, as Anglos and Mexicans alike had something to talk about other than crops and elusive ore. Spencer wondered if this was what it had been like after he had been buffaloed by Greybib Calhoun. Had everyone found his pain and Greybib's comeuppance a reason to howl at the moon? His honor had been sullied that night, and perhaps that was a joke to some. Tonight he would avenge it. He was lucid, sober, and very angry.

Since the fight and the arrest of O'Meara and the four living Hombres, Bendix had been absent. Spencer had checked the livery and found that the familiar roan was in its stall, and the surrey was still parked in the back. If Bendix was alive, he was still in town. He would not have gotten very far on foot; he probably would not even have tried to leave on foot unless he'd panicked. Bendix would be the type to panic, though. No, if the bastard had run, he would have grown cowardly in the desert and would have returned to something familiar. He was a bug as sure as anything, a bug that could be stepped on and crushed. And that was what Spence planned. He was going to crush that man.

The Sam Houston had been filled with Texans and Mexicans, and there had been no hope of finding his adversary there anyway. Bendix stayed so close to O'Meara that Spencer doubted the man had ever been to the Sam Houston. And as for the Nantucket Whaler, Bendix was not foolish enough to show himself in his own bar, not if he was hiding from the law. But he would not have gone far. Quietly, walking on just the heels of his boots, Spencer made his way down the alley beside the bar. It was the picture of absurdity but for the ever-present carbine in his hand.

There was a gasp, someone's attempt at controlling their breathing and foolishly attempting to be quiet. He leveled the big-bore rifle at a wooden crate and cocked the hammer.

"That click rings just as loud as a coin on a table, don't it? Stand up, you villainous bootlicker. Stand or you will stand no more forever."

Bendix's chubby frame rose in the glowing light of the evening. He was bathed in an eerie yellow glow that was singular to the desert at sunset. "What business have you with me, Spence? Have we not always gotten along all right? Your credit has always been good with me."

"Be silent. I have had the chance to study you today. If that bastard boss of yours was tied in with killers, then I suppose that his bootlicker answered to him and for him. Your hiding here puts a stamp of approval on my guess. You are vermin and a bug, and I plan to exact my revenge from you."

Bendix shivered. It was true, his hiding did give the appearance that he was guilty. *No,* he thought, *it is not an appearance but rather a dead giveaway.* Lying had done him no good with O'Meara, but then Spence was not so smart. Perhaps Bendix could convince him to go elsewhere. "Please explain yourself, Spence. If I have worked this bar for him, it has brought no ill your way."

"You villainous son of a bitch, how do you stand there and represent yourself to me? I suppose you would tell me that you had no idea that Greybib Calhoun was coming to Fuerte Viejo. I suppose a man who keeps his environs on the other side of the mountains has little reason to come here. That is, he would not come unless he was called for. I recollect you was in no hurry to get him out, even though he was looking for trouble. I can say he was in bad need of the law's attention, but you did not go, I am told, until after I was buffaloed. My guess is that you brought him here on purpose, and I suppose right. Your face gives you away."

Bendix tried to look incredulous. "Why, Spence, where did you arrive at such a tale? Why on earth would I do such a thing? I run a square house. I have no need to bring in ruffians. You are wrong, sir. Please believe me that you are wrong."

"Before you protest too much, know that O'Meara has been stewing in that hotbox of a jail. Before it swells, a tongue gets mighty loose with thirst. Water works wonders. You may imagine that it would. And I know, sir, that my head paid the fee for that bastard Calhoun. And you, sir, are going to pay me back."

"You are wrong, Spence. Farrell lies. But what do you ask? Just do not shoot me. Do not shoot an innocent man."

"Yeah, an innocent man. I reckon Edwin Brody would love to sit and have a talk with you and me and O'Meara. I suspect that man coming here with two friends whose guns are cocked and ready— why, he would just love to talk to us. You may be a lot heavier dead than alive, if you understand me. What do you reckon the weight of twelve Colt Navy slugs is? But you may live yet if you are willing to sell what part of your soul the devil don't already got."

"What do you mean? What do you want?" Bendix was dizzy. The desert and the town and perhaps his life were all on the periphery of his vision, and he could sense that they would all soon merge into a kaleidoscope of color. He had never fainted before, but he knew that it was imminent.

"You are leaving this burgh and have no need for anything more. Just take your truck and be gone. But before you go, you will sell me this here saloon for one dollar. That, or you can lie here wounded by me until you are killed by Brody. And one more thing. You put yourself on the ground there and taste dirt. Do it right now."

Nodding to allay any further violence, Bendix lowered himself to the ground. The sharp edge of a broken beer bottle pressed into his chest, but he dared not protest. Whatever was to happen was to happen. In just a short moment, perhaps, he would be free. His momentary discomfort was interrupted by something much worse...the warm splash of Spence emptying his bladder.

CHAPTER 76

SATURDAY MORNING

Felipe closed the jailhouse door behind him, muffling the moaning and wailing of the inhabitants within. He absentmindedly used his shirt sleeve to polish the silver stickpin that served as a badge. Brody's old Remington revolver hung in the holster at his waist.

"You look mighty handsome, Mr. Constable," said Verly, perched on the buckboard in front of the jail. She carried a pale blue parasol to shield herself from the harsh sun. It was already broiling despite the early hour.

"Thank you, Miss Harvill. You look very beautiful, *como siempre.* You go safely. How many days to go and come back?"

"It matters not how long we are gone," answered Brody. "You are the representation of law in Fuerte Viejo until you retire or until an election. If you find yourself in need of assistance, you know Peter Heydt and Spence will be here. But you're man enough for the job."

"Thank you, Mr. Edwin. But I will be very happy to see you back."

Brody pulled him closer and whispered, "Let me ask you, Felipe, and there is no shame in it, but is your conscience hurting you? About yesterday, I mean. Are you well?"

"Mr. Edwin, my conscience is very good and strong, because those were bad men. If I do not kill, them they will kill me. And Mr. Edwin, I am American. All of us here are Americans. Those bad men did not belong here. Maybe that does not matter. Maybe that has nothing to do with it. But I want to say it. Anyway, they hurt many people here in Fuerte Viejo. I do not feel badly. So. How many days to go and come back?"

Brody pulled himself onto the buckboard next to Verly, and they both looked back to the second seat, where Banks and Big Sarah sat huddled together. Sarah too was shielded by a parasol. It was dainty and pink and somewhat comical in its attempt to cover her entirety.

"A week is enough time to swear our affidavits with the federal marshal, Felipe," answered Banks. "Until that happens I am sure Judge Fernandez in Santa Ynez would love to address these brigands. Therefore, a week is sufficient. But you do not give us much time for a honeymoon. I suspect we may be gone for a year or more."

"No, a week is good," said Sarah with a giggle. "And that should include plenty of time for me to shop as well. Prescott is big, from what I hear, and I would rather spend the time trading than poking."

Brody popped the reins, and the four horses, good stock from O'Meara's teams, pulled away from in front of the jail. Here and there miners and their families stopped along the boardwalk and waved at the passing wagon. For the first time Brody could remember, everyone looked happy—not the empty and meaningless joy of a single moment, but true inner happiness, peace even. It said much about the tenuous nature of existence in the territory that people could feel so alive when they had faced the death of compatriots just a day previous.

They were out of town before Brody spoke. "McLeroy, can a freed man own property in Arizona?"

"Freed...you mean a Negro? I don't expect the title of freed man is accurate, since there are no slaves. Every man is free now."

"Then can a Negro own land or a title? Spence saw me this morning and said that last night Bendix sold him the Nantucket Whaler for one dollar, the whole thing. And Spence sold Old Abraham half interest for fifty cents. Bendix and his hitch are gone now, and I suspect it is best not to try and find him. If Spence got himself a good deal and both parties are content, then why should I interfere? Felipe is the law now."

Verly smiled, genuinely and from deep within. "Do you mean that, Edwin? You will not seek retribution against Bendix, despite what we now know?"

Brody reached down and grasped Verly's hand with his own. "No, Verly, wherever he is he can stay lodged. If we each stay in our little corners of the world, it is likely that we should never meet. I will not seek him, and he damned sure will not try to find me. More likely he will spend his days in anticipation of my finding him. That kind of punishment, constantly looking over his shoulder and staying on the move, never being able to acquire a big name like he wanted, and never being able to draw attention to himself—well, that is punishment enough for me."

CHAPTER 77

SATURDAY AFTERNOON

To the white people, it was known as Doubtful Canyon, and with very good reason. To the People it was known as Where We Always Kill the Whites. It might have looked like a desolate canyon to an easterner, as it was devoid of any vegetation that would have been found farther west in the Sonoran Desert. To the freighters in Arizona Territory, it looked like a bad but very likely place to die. Ever so frequently stone cairns marked the graves of those wagoneers who had helped give the canyon its name.

To Walking Knife this canyon marked the entranceway to home. For at the end, designated by another larger cairn signifying a line invisible to all but the whites, lay what was called New Mexico Territory and his family group. It meant that home was not far away.

He avoided the highway below and also the ridgetops above, as he would provide a good silhouette to anyone below. Instead he chose a midlevel passage, not too high nor too low. And as he hiked, he found stones moved to serve as rifle pits for his fellow warriors. These pits would be used again and again whenever anyone planned an attack in the canyon. It made him reminisce fondly of the three times he had participated in fights here. Each time had been with his uncle Mangas Colorado and the great Cochise. His uncle was dead, but even now Cochise was wreaking havoc among Mexicans, miners, freighters, and soldiers. Many of the smaller villages in Mexico had ceased to exist, so furious was his assault in that land.

From a distance Walking Knife could see two riders at the end of the canyon. They rode in a small circle off the road and seemed to be investigating something. The more he watched, the more they ambled about, riding somewhat aimlessly but within a confined area. Yes, they were looking for something. They were Inde; even at this distance, it was quite obvious. He pulled his knife and held it aloft, letting the sun catch its sliver blade.

Almost immediately the riders broke for him, and he ran downhill to meet them. The men carried long lances, and their shiny black hair flew behind them as they raced closer. Their features became recognizable as they neared him. Finally he broke into a huge grin. It was Zuni Wife and Silver Horn.

"I am happy to see the sun shine on you, brothers. You see me now after many days of travel. You will see that I am changed. My brothers will not know your old friend."

Zuni Wife and Silver Horn dismounted and hugged their fellow Membreno. "You will see change when you get to our village, Walking Knife. The sad news of our village is good news to you. Gives His Horse Water First made a very fast raid into Chihuahua. He now has a beautiful young Mexican wife that he favors greatly. She favors him greatly too. This wife started a fight with Antelope Under the Moon. Antelope Under the Moon has gone back to her mother. Her brothers are very angry, and the camp is divided. Every person is on one side or the other. But why talk of such matters? This is a problem of the camp. It can wait while we hear about your journey." And there was great laughter between Silver Horn and Zuni Wife.

"Silver Horn, it is no sin to kill one of the People if there is a great wrong. I know this." Walking Knife pulled his namesake once more. He smiled broadly. "You will be my first, and I will skin you if you do not tell me more. What of Antelope Under the Moon? Is their marriage over?"

"Yes, brother. The marriage will be over once you get to the camp. She asks for you."

Walking Knife let out a long and loud scream. Rejuvenated, he leapt upon Silver Horn's mount and galloped eastward, hard and fast. He gave no notice that it left his friend on foot. Or maybe he just did not care.

Silver Horn turned to Zuni Wife and they both laughed. "Our friend says we will not know him after this journey. I say he is the same man. He has the same thoughts he has always had. But after today his name will change. We will no longer call him Walking Knife. He will be known as One-Woman Man."

CHAPTER 78

SATURDAY EVENING

At the McCord ranch, the smell of charred wood was still thick in the air. As Banks readied a campfire, the women prepared blankets and bedding under the wagon. Verly was emotionally and physically drained but went through the motions as best she could. With the wisdom that only a woman could possess, Sarah knew to keep her occupied and as busy as endurance allowed. Meanwhile Brody took one of the newly acquired Winchesters and scouted the area. The Apaches, as he imagined them, were unlikely to double back where they might come into contact with ghosts. However, with so many patrols about, maybe they would be forced to return through this same squalid little ranch. Who really knew what an Apache might do? It was as fruitless as predicting where a leaf would land after having fallen from a tall oak.

Working his way up the same boulder- and rock-strewn hill that he had climbed just two days previous, he paused to look at his companions below and the environment beyond. Behind the ruined cabin, where the woman McCord had been found, there was a clear path that was more like a game trail in its meagerness. It led to a small lean-to that served as an outhouse. It was too small and ill used to have been a kitchen. He would have noticed it before, he guessed, if he had not been preoccupied with the bodies of Pete and the McCords.

Something else caught his attention, a curiosity that, like the trail, or because of it, came to the forefront of his awareness. There was the highway road that was well away but plainly visible from this height. That was a thing of logical existence. Logical too were the trails to the outhouse and to the top of the hill. The McCords would certainly have wanted to use it to observe their surroundings. But from this vantage point, another trail was conspicuous, mysteriously so. It led from the front yard of the cabin to a cleft where this hill joined the next one to the south. What really drew his attention now was that it led to an area devoid of prickly pear, cholla, and the giant saguaros that inhabited every other square patch of soil. Gone too were the inoffensive creosotes and paloverdes. His curiosity now fully aroused, he made his way back down, sliding on the loose shale and stone.

"Edwin, you see something?" Banks had the fire going strong.

Brody looked at the fire and had a momentary thought that what had been a destroyer two days ago was now providing life in the same spot. He shook his head to clear the thought. There was no sense in turning every event into something morose and somber.

"Not yet. I'll be right back."

The trail was now more discernible and proceeded two hundred yards to the cleft, where it ended in a pile of loose rubble sandwiched between two boulders. Various red and yellow pieces of rock as flat and sharp edged as pottery shards covered an area of four feet by four feet.

"Banks, can you hear me?" After several seconds he screamed the question again and was answered by the two shadows of Banks and Verly, elongated by the evening sun. They approached wordlessly, waiting to know what was wrong.

"Is this a footpath to nowhere?" asked Sarah, finally emerging from behind them.

"Folks, does something appear queer, as our old friend Poe would say? This trail to nowhere strikes me as an absurdity."

Verly was the first to respond. "I see it, Edwin. This whole hill is rock and boulder and cactus. But right here…" She approached the specific area. "This right here is nothing but small stone. I do believe it is just a concealment for something else. This is unnatural."

Banks and Sarah met Brody's eyes and nodded to show that they agreed. For several moments they stood and looked at their discovery. Finally, perhaps as much to break the tension as for curiosity, Brody took his rifle and used the butt stock to clear the loose rubble. In a short moment, his rifle sounded on wood, and Sarah and Banks joined in with their bare hands, revealing several flat boards joined together as if to form a door. With no more words between them, Brody grabbed the door and flung it away to uncover a gaping hole. Deep and cavernous, it could be only one thing.

"My goodness, Edwin," said Verly, clasping her hands together in anticipation. "What others have spent months and years searching for, you have uncovered in a moment. The Lost Treasure of Fuerte Viejo."

There were smiles all around, but Edwin let out a sigh, a sigh so deep and long it could have only been preceded by the biggest breath ever. "Let's cover it back up. I am not sure that I want it."

There was no reply from anyone, so he continued. "If we change our minds, it is here. But we don't know who this belongs to, if anyone. Maybe I would like to see Felipe and the others get a share. I don't know. But, Verly, if you will be with me, I think I can be happy without it. Can you?"

She smiled. "I can, Edwin. I can. Let's cover this up."

The other couple looked in astonishment and finally shrugged, their bewilderment momentarily too much for words. Banks knelt down in the stones and began to cover the wooden door. "Come on and help me. Living by your wits is apt to be more fun anyhow."

Thanks to Marshall Trimble for his patience and to Elaine McGee, Sandra Tullis, and Dr. Anne Crane for their encouragement